"Don't [...]
Self-consci[...]

Rett said quietly. "I know you've never let another man touch you like that."

She stared at him, eyes widening. Of all the things she'd expected he might say, that wasn't one of them.

His nostrils flared. "After supper," he said slowly, holding her eyes, "I'm going to carry you into the living room and I'm going to make love to you, in every way I know. And when I get through, you'll shudder at the thought of another man's hands on you."

DIANA PALMER

is a native Georgian and a former newspaper reporter. She married her husband, James, after a five-day courtship, and they now have a young son. They are still newlyweds, having been married only eleven years. They live with two arrogant Siamese cats in a small northeast Georgia town, where Ms. Palmer spends her free time planting flowers, running her electric trains, and chasing unicorns.

Dear Reader:

I'd like to take this opportunity to thank you for all your support and encouragement of Silhouette Romances.

Many of you write in regularly, telling us what you like best about Silhouette, which authors are your favorites. This is a tremendous help to us as we strive to publish the best contemporary romances possible.

All the romances from Silhouette Books are for you, so enjoy this book and the many stories to come.

Karen Solem
Editor-in-Chief
Silhouette Books

DIANA PALMER
Passion Flower

Silhouette Romance

Published by Silhouette Books New York

America's Publisher of Contemporary Romance

To Victoria, Texas, with love

SILHOUETTE BOOKS, a Division of Simon & Schuster, Inc.
1230 Avenue of the Americas, New York, N.Y. 10020

Distributed by Pocket Books

ISBN: 0-671-57328-4

First Silhouette Books printing November, 1984

10 9 8 7 6 5 4 3 2 1

Map by Ray Lundgren

America's Publisher of Contemporary Romance

Printed in the U.S.A.

BC91

Books by Diana Palmer

Silhouette Romance

Darling Enemy #254
Roomful of Roses #301
Heart of Ice #314
Passion Flower #328

Silhouette Special Edition

Heather's Song #33

Silhouette Desire

The Cowboy and the Lady #12
September Morning #26
Friends and Lovers #50
Fire and Ice #80
Snow Kisses #102
Diamond Girl #110
The Rawhide Man #157
Lady Love #175

OKLAHOMA

NEW MEXICO

ARK.

L. A.

N
W · E
S

Fort Worth ● ● Dallas

TEXAS

Houston ●

San Antonio ● *Big Spur*

Branntville ●

Victoria ●

MEXICO

GULF OF
MEXICO

TEXAS

Places in _italics_ are fictitious.

Chapter One

Jennifer King eyed the closed hotel room door nervously. She hadn't wanted this assignment, but she hadn't had much choice, either. Her recent illness had left her savings account bare, and this job was all she had to hold on to. It was a long way from the brilliant career in interior decorating she'd left behind in New York. But it was a living.

She pushed back a loose strand of blond hair and hoped she looked sedate enough for the cattleman behind the door. The kind of clothes she'd favored in New York were too expensive for her budget in Atlanta.

She knocked at the door and waited. It seemed to take forever for the man inside to get there. Finally, without warning, the door swung open.

"Miss King?" he asked, smiling pleasantly.

She smiled back. He was much younger than she'd expected him to be. Tall and fair and pleasant. "Yes," she said. "You rang for a temporary secretary?"

"Just need a few letters done, actually," he said, taking the heavy portable typewriter from her hand. "I'm buying some cattle for my brother."

"Yes, Miss James at the agency told me it had to do with cattle." She sat down quickly. She was pale and wan, still feeling the after-effects of a terrible bout with pneumonia.

"Say, are you all right?" he asked, frowning.

"Fine, thank you, Mr. Culhane," she said, remembering his name from Miss James's description of the job. "I'm just getting over pneumonia, and I'm a little weak."

He sat down across from her on the sofa, lean and rangy, and smiled. "I guess it does take the whip out of you. I've never had it myself, but Everett nearly died on us one year. He smokes too much," he confided.

"Your brother?" she asked with polite interest as she got her steno pad and pen from her large purse.

"My brother. The senior partner. Everett runs the show." He sounded just a little jealous. She glanced up. Jennifer was twenty-three, and he couldn't have been much older. She felt a kinship with him. Until their deaths three years back, her parents had pretty much nudged her into the job they thought she wanted. By the sound of it,

Everett Culhane had done the same with this young man.

She dug out her pad and pen and crossed her thin legs. All of her was thin. Back in New York, before the frantic pace threatened her health, she'd been slender and poised and pretty enough to draw any man's eye. But now she was only a pale wraith, a ghost of the woman she'd been. Her blond hair was brittle and lusterless, her pale green eyes were dull, without their old sparkle. She looked bad, and that fact registered in the young man's eyes.

"Are you sure you feel up to this?" he asked gently. "You don't look well."

"I'm a little frail, that's all," she replied proudly. "I'm only just out of the hospital, you see."

"I guess that's why," he muttered. He got up, pacing the room, and found some notes scribbled on lined white paper. "Well, this first letter goes to Everett Culhane, Circle C Ranch, Big Spur, Texas."

"Texas?" Her pale eyes lit up. "Really?"

His eyebrows lifted, and he grinned. "Really. The town is named after a king-sized ranch nearby —the Big Spur. It's owned by Cole Everett and his wife Heather, and their three sons. Our ranch isn't a patch on that one, but big brother has high hopes."

"I've always wanted to see a real cattle ranch," she confided. "My grandfather went cowboying out to Texas as a boy. He used to talk about it all the time, about the places he'd seen, and the history . . ." She sat up straight, poising her pen over the pad. "Sorry. I didn't mean to get off the track."

"That's all right. Funny, you don't look like a girl who'd care for the outdoors," he commented as he sat back down with the sheaf of papers in his hand.

"I love it," she said quietly. "I lived in a small town until I was ten and my parents moved to Atlanta. I missed it terribly. I still do."

"Can't you go back?" he asked.

She shook her head sadly. "It's too late. I have no family left. My parents are dead. There are a few scattered relatives, but none close enough to visit."

"That's rough. Kind of like me and Everett," he added. "We got raised by our aunt and uncle. At least, I did. Everett wasn't so lucky. Our dad was still alive while he was a boy." His face clouded, as if with an unpleasant memory. He cleared his throat. "Well, anyway, back to the letter . . ."

He began to dictate, and she kept up with him easily. He thought out the sentences before he gave them to her, so there were few mistakes or changes. She wondered why he didn't just call his brother, but she didn't ask the question. She took down several pages of description about bulls and pedigrees and bloodlines. There was a second letter, to a bank executive in Big Spur, detailing the method the Culhane brothers had devised to pay back a sizeable loan. The third letter was to a breeder in Carrollton, outlining transport for a bull the man had evidently purchased from the Culhanes.

"Confused?" he murmured dryly when he stopped.

"It's not my business . . ." she began gently.

"We're selling off one of our best bulls," he said, "to give us enough down payment on another top breeding bull. Everett is trying for a purebred Hereford herd. But we don't have the cash, so I've come down here to do some fancy trading. I sold the bull we had. Now I'm trying to get a potential seller to come down on his price."

"Wouldn't a phone call to your brother be quicker?" she asked.

"Sure. And Everett would skin my head. I came out here on a bus, for God's sake, instead of a plane. We're just about mortgaged to the hilt, you see. Everett says we can't afford not to pinch pennies." His eyes twinkled. "We've got Highland Scots in our ancestry, you see."

She smiled. "Yes, I suppose so. I can see his point. Phone calls are expensive."

"Especially the kind it would take to relay this much information," he agreed, nodding toward what he'd dictated. "If I get it off today, he'll have it in a day or two. Then, if he thinks it's worth giving what the man wants, he can call me and just say a word or two. In the meantime, I've got other business to attend to."

"Shrewd idea," she murmured.

"Just a couple more," he continued. He leaned back and studied a magazine. "Okay, this one goes to . . ." He gave her a name and address in north Georgia, and dictated a letter asking if the breeder could give him a call at the hotel on Friday at 1 P.M. Then he dictated a second letter to a breeder in south Georgia, making the same request for 2 P.M. He grinned at her faint smile.

"Saving money," he assured her. "Although why Everett wants to do it the hard way is beyond me. There's a geologist who swears we've got one hell of a lot of oil on our western boundary, but Everett dug in his heels and refused to sell off the drilling rights. Even for a percentage. Can you beat that? We could be millionaires, and here I sit writing letters asking people to call me, just to save money."

"Why won't he sell?" she asked, curious.

"Because he's a purist," he grumbled. "He doesn't want to spoil the land. He'd rather struggle to make the cattle pay. Fat chance. The way things have been going, we're going to wind up eating those damned purebreds, papers and all."

She laughed helplessly at his phrasing and hid her face in her hand. "Sorry," she mumbled. "I didn't mean to laugh."

"It is kind of funny," he confessed. "But not when you're cutting corners like we are."

She got up and started to lift the typewriter onto the desk by the window, struggling with it.

"Here, let me do that," he said, and put it onto

the flat surface for her. "You're pretty weak, little lady."

"I'm getting back on my feet," she assured him. "Just a little wobbly, that's all."

"Well, I'll leave you to it. I'm going down to get a sandwich. Can I bring you something?"

She'd have loved a sandwich, but she wasn't going to put any further drain on his resources. "No, thank you," she said, politely and with a smile. "I just had lunch before I came over here."

"Okay, then. See you in a half hour or so."

He jammed a straw cowboy hat on his head and went out the door, closing it softly behind him.

Jennifer typed the letters quickly and efficiently, even down to the cattle's pedigrees. It was a good thing she'd taken that typing course when she was going through the school of interior design in New York, she thought. It had come in handy when the pressure of competition laid her out. She wasn't ready to handle that competitive rat race again yet. She needed to rest, and by comparison typing letters for out-of-town businessmen was a piece of cake.

She felt oddly sorry for this businessman, and faintly sympathetic with his brother, who'd rather go spare than sell out on his principles. She wondered if he looked like his younger brother.

Her eyes fell on the name she was typing at the bottom of the letter. Robert G. Culhane. That must be the man who'd dictated them. He seemed to know cattle, from his meticulous description of them. Her eyes wandered over what looked like a production record for a herd sire, and she sighed. Texas and cattle. She wondered what the Circle C Ranch was like, and while she finished up the letters, lost herself in dreams of riding horseback over flat plains. Pipe dreams, she thought, smiling as she stacked the neat letters with their accompanying envelopes. She'd never see Texas.

Just as she rose from the typewriter, the door opened, and Robert Culhane was back. He smiled at her.

"Taking a break?" he asked as he swept off his hat and whirled it onto a table.

"No, I'm finished," she said, astounding him.

"Already?" He grabbed up the letters and bent over the desk, proofreading them one by one and shaking his head. "Damn, you're fast."

"I do around a hundred words a minute," she replied. "It's one of my few talents."

"You'd be a godsend at the ranch," he sighed. "It takes Everett an hour to type one letter. He cusses a blue streak when he has to write anything on that infernal old machine. And there are all the production records we have to keep, and the tax records, and the payroll . . ." His head lifted and he frowned. "I don't suppose you'd like a job?"

She caught her breath. "In Texas?"

"You make it sound like a religious experience," he murmured on a laugh.

"You can't imagine how much I hate the city," she replied, brushing back a strand of dull hair. "I still cough all the time because of the pollution, and the apartment where I live has no space at all. I'd almost work for free just to be out in the country."

He cocked his head at her and pursed his boyish lips. "It wouldn't be easy, working for Everett," he said. "And you'd have to manage your own fare to Big Spur. You see, I'll need a little time to convince him. You'd barely get minimum wage. And knowing Everett, you'd wind up doing a lot of things besides typing. We don't have a housekeeper . . ."

Her face lit up. "I can make curtains and cook."

"Do you have a telephone?"

She sighed. "No."

"Kind of in the same boat we are in, aren't you?" he said with a sympathetic smile. "I'm Robert Culhane, by the way."

"Jennifer King," she said for the second time that day, and extended her hand.

"Nice to meet you, Jenny. How can I reach you?"

"The agency will take a message for me," she said.

"Fine. I'll be in town for several more days. I'll be in touch with you before I go back to Texas. Okay?"

She beamed. "You're really serious?"

"I'm really serious. And this is great work," he added, gesturing toward the letters. "Jenny, it won't be an easy life on the Circle C. It's nothing like those fancy ranches you see on television."

"I'm not expecting it to be," she said honestly,

and was picturing a ramshackle house that needed paint and curtains and overhauling, and two lonely men living in it. She smiled. "I'm just expecting to be needed."

"You'll be that," he sighed, staring at her critically. "But are you up to hard work?"

"I'll manage," she promised. "Being out in the open, in fresh air, will make me strong. Besides, it'll be dry air out there, and it's summer."

"You'll burn up in the heat," he promised.

"I burn up in the heat here," she said. "Atlanta is a southern city. We get hundred-degree temperatures here."

"Just like home," he murmured with a smile.

"I'd like to come," she said as she got her purse and closed up the typewriter. "But I don't want to get you into any trouble with your brother."

"Everett and I hardly ever have anything except trouble," he said easily. "Don't worry about me. You'd be doing us a big favor. I'll talk Everett into it."

"Should I write you another letter?" She hesitated.

He shook his head. "I'll have it out with him when I get home," he said. "No sweat. Thanks for doing my letters. I'll send the agency a check, you tell them."

"I will. And thank you!"

She hardly felt the weight of the typewriter on her way back to the agency. She was floating on a cloud.

Miss James gave her a hard look when she came back in. "You're late," she said. "We had to refuse a call."

"I'm sorry. There were several letters . . ." she began.

"You've another assignment. Here's the address. A politician. Wants several copies of a speech he's giving, to hand out to the press. You're to type the speech and get it photostatted for him."

She took the outstretched address and sighed. "The typewriter . . . ?"

"He has his own, an electric one. Leave that one here, if you please." Miss James buried her silver head in paperwork. "You may go home when you finish. I'll see you in the morning. Good night."

"Good night," Jennifer said quietly, sighing as she went out onto the street. It would be well after quitting time when she finished, and Miss James knew it. But perhaps the politician would be generous enough to tip her. If only the Texas job worked out! Jennifer was a scrapper when she was at her peak, but she was weary and sick and dragged out. It wasn't a good time to get into an argument with the only employer she'd been able to find. All the other agencies were overstaffed with out-of-work people begging for any kind of job.

The politician was a city councilman, in a good mood and very generous. Jennifer treated herself to three hamburgers and two cups of coffee on the way back to her small apartment. It was in a private home, and dirt cheap. The landlady wasn't overly friendly, but it was a roof over her head and the price was right.

She slept fitfully, dreaming about the life she'd left behind in New York. It all seemed like something out of a fantasy. The competition for the plum jobs, the cocktail parties to make contacts, the deadlines, the endless fighting to land the best accounts, the agonizing perfecting of color schemes and coordinating pieces to fit fussy tastes . . . Her nerves had given out, and then her body.

It hadn't been her choice to go to New York. She'd have been happy in Atlanta. But the best schools were up north, and her parents had insisted. They wanted her to have the finest training available, so she let herself be gently pushed. Two years after she graduated, they were dead. She'd never truly gotten over their deaths in the plane crash. They'd been on their way to a party on Christmas Eve. The plane went down in the dark, in a lake, and it had been hours before they were missed.

In the two years since her graduation, Jennifer had landed a job at one of the top interior-decoration businesses in the city. She'd pushed herself over the limit to get clients, going to impossible lengths to please them. The outcome had been inevitable. Pneumonia landed her in the hospital for several days in March, and she was too drained to go back to work immediately after. An up-and-coming young designer had stepped neatly

into her place, and she had found herself suddenly
without work.

Everything had to go, of course. The luxury
apartment, the furs, the designer clothes. She'd
sold them all and headed south. Only to find that
the job market was overloaded and she couldn't
find a job that wouldn't finish killing her. Except at
a temporary agency, where she could put her
typing skills to work. She started working for Miss
James, and trying to recover. But so far she'd failed
miserably. And now the only bright spot in her
future was Texas.

She prayed as she never had before, struggling
from one assignment to the next and hoping beyond hope that the phone call would come. Late
one Friday afternoon, it did. And she happened to
be in the office when it came.

"Miss King?" Robert Culhane asked on a laugh.
"Still want to go to Texas?"

"Oh, yes!" she said fervently, holding tightly to
the telephone cord.

"Then pack a bag and be at the ranch bright and
early a week from Monday morning. Got a pencil?
Okay, here's how to get there."

She was so excited she could barely scribble. She
got down the directions. "I can't believe it, it's like
a dream!" she said enthusiastically. "I'll do a good
job, really I will. I won't be any trouble, and the
pay doesn't matter!"

"I'll tell Everett," he chuckled. "Don't forget.

You needn't call. Just come on out to the ranch. I'll be there to smooth things over with old Everett, okay?"

"Okay. Thank you!"

"Thank *you,* Miss King," he said. "See you a week from Monday."

"Yes, sir!" She hung up, her face bright with hope. She was actually going to Texas!

"Miss King?" Miss James asked suspiciously.

"Oh! I won't be back in after today, Miss James," she said politely. "Thank you for letting me work with you. I've enjoyed it very much."

Miss James looked angry. "You can't just walk out like this," she said.

"But I can," Jennifer said, with some of her old spirit. She picked up her purse. "I didn't sign a contract, Miss James. And if you were to push the point, I'd tell you that I worked a great deal of overtime for which I wasn't paid," she added with a pointed stare. "How would you explain that to the people down at the state labor department?"

Miss James stiffened. "You're ungrateful."

"No, I'm not. I'm very grateful. But I'm leaving, all the same. Good day." She nodded politely just before she went out, and closed the door firmly behind her.

Chapter Two

It was blazing hot for a spring day in Texas. Jennifer stopped in the middle of the ranch road to rest for a minute and set her burdens down on the dusty, graveled ground. She wished for the tenth time in as many minutes that she'd let the cab driver take her all the way to the Culhanes' front door. But she'd wanted to walk. It hadn't seemed a long way from the main road. And it was so beautiful, with the wildflowers strewn across the endless meadows toward the flat horizon. Bluebonnets, which she'd only read about until then, and Mexican hat and Indian paintbrush. Even the names of the flowers were poetic. But her enthusiasm had outweighed her common sense. And her strength.

She'd tried to call the ranch from town—apparently Everett and Robert Culhane did have the luxury of a telephone. But it rang and rang with no answer. Well, it was Monday, and she'd been promised a job. She hefted her portable typewriter and her suitcase and started out again.

Her pale eyes lifted to the house in the distance. It was a two-story white frame building, with badly peeling paint and a long front porch. Towering live oaks protected it from the sun, trees bigger than anything Jennifer had seen in Georgia. And the feathery green trees with the crooked trunks had to be mesquite. She'd never seen it, but she'd done her share of reading about it.

On either side of the long, graveled driveway were fences, gray with weathering and strung with rusting barbed wire. Red-coated cattle grazed behind the fences, and her eyes lingered on the wide horizon. She'd always thought Georgia was big—until now. Texas was just unreal. In a separate pasture, a mare and her colt frolicked in the hot sun.

Jennifer pushed back a strand of dull blond hair that had escaped from her bun. In a white shirt-waist dress and high heels, she was a strange sight to be walking up the driveway of a cattle ranch. But she'd wanted to make a good impression.

Her eyes glanced down ruefully at the red dust on the hem of her dress, and the scuff marks on her last good pair of white sling pumps. She could have cried. One of her stockings had run, and she was sweating. She could hardly have looked worse if she'd planned it.

She couldn't help being a little nervous about the older brother. She had Everett Culhane pictured as a staid old rancher with a mean temper. She'd met businessmen like that before, and dealt with them. She wasn't afraid of him. But she hoped that he'd be glad of her help. It would make things easier all around.

Her footsteps echoed along the porch as she walked up the worn steps. She would have looked around more carefully weeks ago, but now she was tired and run down and just too exhausted to care what her new surroundings looked like.

She paused at the screen door, and her slender fingers brushed the dust from her dress. She put the suitcase and the typewriter down, took a steadying breath, and knocked.

There was no sound from inside the house. The wooden door was standing open, and she thought she heard the whir of a fan. She knocked again. Maybe it would be the nice young man she'd met in Atlanta who would answer the door. She only hoped she was welcome.

The sound of quick, hard footsteps made her heart quicken. Someone was home, at least. Maybe she could sit down. She was feeling a little faint.

"Who the hell are you?" came a harsh masculine voice from behind the screen door, and Jennifer looked up into the hardest face and the coldest dark eyes she'd ever seen.

She couldn't even find her voice. Her immediate

reaction was to turn around and run for it. But she'd come too far, and she was too tired.

"I'm Jennifer King," she said as professionally as she could. "Is Robert Culhane home, please?"

She was aware of the sudden tautening of his big body, a harsh intake of breath, before she looked up and saw the fury in his dark eyes.

"What the hell kind of game are you playing, lady?" he demanded.

She stared at him. It had been a long walk, and now it looked as if she might have made a mistake and come to the wrong ranch. Her usual confidence faltered. "Is this the Circle C ranch?" she asked.

"Yes, it is."

He wasn't forthcoming, and she wondered if he might be one of the hired hands. "Is this where Robert Culhane lives?" she persisted, trying to peek past him—there was a lot of him, all hard muscle and blue denim.

"Bobby was killed in a bus wreck a week ago," he said harshly.

Jennifer was aware of a numb feeling in her legs. The long trip on the bus, the heavy suitcase, the effects of her recent illness—all of it added up to exhaustion. And those cold words were the final blow. With a pitiful little sound, she sank down onto the porch, her head whirling, nausea running up into her throat like warm water.

The screen door flew open and a pair of hard, impatient arms reached down to lift her. She felt herself effortlessly carried, like a sack of flour, into the cool house. She was unceremoniously dumped down onto a worn brocade sofa and left there while booted feet stomped off into another room. There were muttered words that she was glad she couldn't understand, and clinking sounds. Then, a minute later, a glass of dark amber liquid was held to her numb lips and a hard hand raised her head.

She sipped at the cold, sweet iced tea like a runner on the desert when confronted with wet salvation. She struggled to catch her breath and sat up, gently nudging the dark, lean hand holding the glass to one side. She breathed in deeply, trying to get her whirling mind to slow down. She was still trying to take it all in. She'd been promised a job, she'd come hundreds of miles at her own expense to work for minimum wage, and now the man who'd offered it to her was dead. That was the worst part, imagining such a nice young man dead.

"You look like a bleached handkerchief," the deep, harsh voice observed.

She sighed. "You ought to write for television. You sure do have a gift for prose."

His dark eyes narrowed. "Walking in this heat without a hat. My God, how many stupid city women are there in the world? And what landed you on my doorstep?"

She lifted her eyes then, to look at him properly. He was darkly tanned, and there were deep lines in his face, from the hatchet nose down to the wide, chiseled mouth. His eyes were deep-set, unblinking under heavy dark brows and a wide forehead. His hair was jet-black, straight and thick and a little shaggy. He was wearing what had to be work clothes: faded denim jeans that emphasized long, powerfully muscled legs, and a matching shirt whose open neck revealed a brown chest thick with short, curling hair. He had the look of a man who was all business, all the time. All at once she realized that this man wasn't the hired hand she'd mistaken him for.

"You're Everett Culhane," she said hesitantly.

His face didn't move. Not a muscle in it changed position, but she had the distinct feeling that the sound of his name on her lips had shocked him.

She took another long sip of the tea and sighed at the pleasure of the icy liquid going down her parched throat.

"How far did you walk?" he asked.

"Just from the end of your driveway," she admitted, looking down at her ruined shoes. "Distance is deceptive out here."

"Haven't you ever heard of sunstroke?"

She nodded. "It just didn't occur to me."

She put the glass down on the napkin he'd brought with it. Well, this was Texas. How sad that she wouldn't see anything more of it.

"I'm very sorry about your brother, Mr. Culhane," she said with dignity. "I didn't know him very well, but he seemed like a nice man." She got up with an odd kind of grace despite the unsteadiness of her legs. "I won't take up any more of your time."

"Why did you come, Miss King?"

She shook her head. "It doesn't matter now in the least." She turned and went out the screen door, lifting her suitcase and typewriter from where they'd fallen when she fainted. It was going to be a long walk back to town, but she'd just have to manage it. She had bus fare back home and a little more. A cab was a luxury now, with no job at the end of her long ride.

"Where do you think you're going?" Everett Culhane asked from behind her, his tone like a whiplash.

"Back to town," she said without turning. "Good-bye, Mr. Culhane."

"Walking?" he mused. "In this heat, without a hat?"

"Got here, didn't I?" she drawled as she walked down the steps.

"You'll never make it back. Wait a minute. I'll drive you."

"No, thanks," she said proudly. "I get around all right by myself, Mr. Culhane. I don't need any handouts."

"You'll need a doctor if you try that walk," he said, and turned back into the house.

She thought the matter was settled, until a battered red pickup truck roared up beside her and stopped. The passenger door flew open.

"Get in," he said curtly, in a tone that made it clear he expected instant obedience.

"I said . . ." she began irritatedly.

His dark eyes narrowed. "I don't mind lifting you in and holding you down until we get to town," he said quietly.

With a grimace, she climbed in, putting the typewriter and suitcase on the floorboard.

There was a marked lack of conversation. Everett smoked his cigarette with sharp glances in her direction when she began coughing. Her lungs were still sensitive, and he seemed to be smoking shucks or something equally potent. Eventually he crushed out the cigarette and cracked a window.

"You don't sound well," he said suddenly.

"I'm getting over pneumonia," she said, staring lovingly at the horizon. "Texas sure is big."

"It sure is." He glanced at her. "Which part of it do you call home?"

"I don't."

The truck lurched as he slammed on the brakes. "What did you say?"

"I'm not a Texan," she confessed. "I'm from Atlanta."

"Georgia?"

"Is there another one?"

He let out a heavy breath. "What the hell did you mean, coming this distance just to see a man you hardly knew?" he burst out. "Surely to God, it wasn't love at first sight?"

"Love?" She blinked. "Heavens, no. I only did some typing for your brother."

He cut off the engine. "Start over. Start at the

beginning. You're giving me one hell of a headache. How did you wind up out here?"

"Your brother offered me a job," she said quietly. "Typing. Of course, he said there'd be other
duties as well. Cooking, cleaning, things like that.
And a very small salary." she added with a tiny
smile.

"He was honest with you, at least," he growled.
"But then why did you come? Didn't you believe
him?"

"Yes, of course," she said hesitantly. "Why
wouldn't I want to come?"

He started to light another cigarette, stared hard
at her, and put the pack back in his shirt pocket.
"Keep talking."

He was an odd man, she thought. "Well, I'd lost
my old job, because once I got over the pneumonia
I was too weak to keep up the pace. I got a job in
Atlanta with one of the temporary talent agencies
doing typing. My speed is quite good, and it was
something that didn't wring me out, you see. Mr.
Culhane wanted some letters typed. We started
talking," she smiled, remembering how kind he'd
been, "and when I found out he was from Texas,
from a real ranch, I guess I just went crazy. I've
spent my whole life listening to my grandfather
relive his youth in Texas, Mr. Culhane. I've read
everything Zane Grey and Louis Lamour ever
wrote, and it was the dream of my life to come out
here. The end of the rainbow. I figured that a low

salary on open land would be worth a lot more than a big salary in the city, where I was choking to death on smog and civilization. He offered me the job and I said yes on the spot." She glanced at him ruefully. "I'm not usually so slow. But I was feeling so bad, and it sounded so wonderful . . . I didn't even think about checking with you first. Mr. Culhane said he'd have it all worked out, and that I was just to get on a bus and come on out today." Her eyes clouded. "I'm so sorry about him. Losing the job isn't nearly as bad as hearing that he . . . was killed. I liked him."

Everett's fingers were tapping an angry pattern on the steering wheel. "A job." He laughed mirthlessly, then sighed. "Well, maybe he had a point. I'm so behind on my production records and tax records, it isn't funny. I'm choking to death on my own cooking, the house hasn't been swept in a month . . . " He glanced at her narrowly. "You aren't pregnant?"

Her pale eyes flashed at him. "That, sir, would make medical history."

One dark eyebrow lifted and he glanced at her studiously before he smiled. "Little Southern lady, are you really that innocent?"

"Call me Scarlett and, unemployment or no unemployment, I'll paste you one, cowboy," she returned with a glimmer of her old spirit. It was too bad that the outburst triggered a coughing spree.

"Damn," he muttered, passing her his handkerchief. "All right, I'll stop baiting you. Do you want the job, or don't you? Robert was right about the wages. You'll get bed and board free, but it's going to be a frugal existence. Interested?"

"If it means getting to stay in Texas, yes, I am."

He smiled. "How old are you, schoolgirl?"

"I haven't been a schoolgirl for years, Mr. Culhane," she told him. "I'm twenty-three, in fact." She glared at him. "How old are you?"

"Make a guess," he invited.

Her eyes went from his thick hair down the hawklike features to his massive chest, which tapered to narrow hips, long powerful legs, and large, booted feet. "Thirty," she said.

He chuckled softly. It was the first time she'd heard the deep, pleasant sound, and it surprised her to find that he was capable of laughter. He didn't seem like the kind of man who laughed very often.

His eyes wandered over her thin body with amused indifference, and she regretted for a minute that she was such a shadow of her former self. "Try again, honey," he said.

She noticed then the deep lines in his darkly tanned face, the sprinkling of gray hair at his temples. In the open neck of his shirt, she could see threads of silver among the curling dark hair. No, he wasn't as young as she'd first thought.

"Thirty-four," she guessed.

"Add a year and you've got it."

She smiled. "Poor old man," she said with gentle humor.

He chuckled again. "That's no way to talk to your new boss," he cautioned.

"I won't forget again, honestly." She stared at him. "Do you have other people working for you?"

"Just Eddie and Bib," he said. "They're married." He nodded as he watched her eyes become wide and apprehensive. "That's right. We'll be alone. I'm a bachelor and there's no staff in the house."

"Well . . ."

"There'll be a lock on your door," he said after a minute. "When you know me better, you'll see that I'm pretty conventional in my outlook. It's a big house. We'll rattle around like two peas in a pod. It's only on rare occasions that I'm in before bedtime." His dark eyes held hers. "And for the record, my taste doesn't run to city girls."

That sounded as if there was a good reason for his taste in women, but she didn't pry. "I'll work hard, Mr. Culhane."

"My name is Everett," he said, watching her. "Or Rett, if you prefer. You can cook meals and do the laundry and housekeeping. And when you have time, you can work in what passes for my office. Wages won't be much. I can pay the bills, and that's about it."

"I don't care about getting rich." Meanwhile she was thinking fast, sorely tempted to accept the offer, but afraid of the big, angry man at her side. There were worse things than being alone and without money, and she didn't really know him at all.

He saw the thoughts in her mind. "Jenny Wren," he said softly, "do I look like a mad rapist?"

Hearing her name that way on his lips sent a surge of warmth through her. No one had called her by a pet name since the death of her parents.

"No," she said quietly. "Of course you don't. I'll work for you, Mr. Culhane."

He didn't answer her. He only scanned her face and nodded. Then he started the truck, turned it around, and headed back to the Circle C Ranch.

Chapter Three

Two hours later, Jennifer was well and truly in residence, to the evident amusement of Everett's two ranchhands. They apparently knew better than to make any snide comments about her presence, but they did seem to find something fascinating about having a young woman around the place.

Jennifer had her own room, with peeling wallpaper, worn blue gingham curtains at the windows, and a faded quilt on the bed. Most of the house was like that. Even the rugs on the floor were faded and worn from use. She'd have given anything to be robust and healthy and have a free hand to redecorate the place. It had such wonderful potential with its long history and simple, uncluttered architecture.

The next morning she slept late, rising to bright

sunlight and a strange sense that she belonged there. She hadn't felt that way since her childhood, and couldn't help wondering why. Everett had been polite, but not much more. He wasn't really a welcoming kind of man. But, then, he'd just lost his brother. That must account for his taciturn aloofness.

He was long gone when she went downstairs. She fixed herself a cup of coffee and two pieces of toast and then went to the small room that doubled as his office. As he'd promised the day before, he'd laid out a stack of production records and budget information that needed typing. He'd even put her electric typewriter on a table and plugged it in. There was a stack of white paper beside it, and a note.

"Don't feel obliged to work yourself into a coma the first day," it read. And his bold signature was slashed under the terse sentence. She smiled at the flowing handwriting and the perfect spelling. He was a literate man, at least.

She sat down in her cool blue shirtwaist dress and got to work. Two hours later, she'd made great inroads into the paperwork and was starting a new sheet when Everett's heavy footsteps resounded throughout the house. The door swung open and his dark eyebrown shot straight up.

"Aren't you going to eat lunch?" he asked.

More to the point, wasn't she going to feed him, she thought, and grinned.

"Something funny, Miss King?" he asked.

"Oh, no, boss," she said, leaving the typewriter behind. He was expecting that she'd forgotten his noon meal, but she had a surprise in store for him.

She led him into the kitchen, where two places were set. He stood there staring at the table, scowling, while she put out bread, mayonnaise, some thick ham she'd found in the refrigerator, and a small salad she'd made with a bottled dressing.

"Coffee?" she asked, poised with the pot in her hand.

He nodded, sliding into the place at the head of the table.

She poured it into his thick white mug and then filled her own.

"How did you know I wanted coffee instead of tea?" he asked with a narrow gaze as she seated herself beside him.

"Because the coffee canister was half empty and the tea had hardly been touched," she replied with a smile.

He chuckled softly as he sipped the black liquid. "Not bad," he murmured, glancing at her.

"I'm sorry about breakfast," she said. "I usually wake up around six, but this morning I was kind of tired."

"No problem," he told her, reaching for bread. "I'm used to getting my own breakfast."

"What do you have?"

"Coffee."

She gaped at him. "Coffee?"

He shrugged. "Eggs bounce, bacon's half raw,

and the toast hides under some black stuff. Coffee's better."

Her eyes danced as she put some salad on her plate. "I guess so. I'll try to wake up on time tomorrow."

"Don't rush it," he said, glancing at her with a slight frown. "You look puny to me."

"Most people would look puny compared to you," she replied.

"Have you always been that thin?" he persisted.

"No. Not until I got pneumonia," she said. "I just went straight downhill. I suppose I just kept pushing too hard. It caught up with me."

"How's the paperwork coming along?"

"Oh, I'm doing fine," she said. "Your handwriting is very clear. I've had some correspondence to type for doctors that required translation."

"Who did you get to translate?"

She grinned. "The nearest pharmacist. They have experience, you see."

He smiled at her briefly before he bit into his sandwich. He made a second one, but she noticed that he ignored the salad.

"Don't you want some of this?" she asked, indicating the salad bowl.

"I'm not a rabbit," he informed her.

"It's very good for you."

"So is liver, I'm told, but I won't eat that either." He finished his sandwich and got up to pour himself another cup of coffee.

"Then why do you keep lettuce and tomatoes?"

He glanced at her. "I like it on sandwiches."

This was a great time to tell her, after she'd used it all up in the salad. Just like a man . . .

"You could have dug it out of here," she said weakly.

He cocked an eyebrow. "With salad dressing all over it?"

"You could scrape it off . . ."

"I don't like broccoli or cauliflower, and never fix creamed beef," he added. "I'm more or less a meat and potatoes man."

"I'll sure remember that from now on, Mr. Culhane," she promised. "I'll be careful to use potatoes instead of apples in the pie I'm fixing for supper."

He glared at her. "Funny girl. Why don't you go on the stage?"

"Because you'd starve to death and weigh heavily on my conscience," she promised. "Some man named Brickmayer called and asked did you have a farrier's hammer he could borrow." she glanced up. "What's a farrier?"

He burst out laughing. "A farrier is a man who shoes horses."

"I'd like a horse," she sighed. "I'd put him in saddle oxfords."

"Go back to work. But slowly," he added from the doorway. "I don't want you knocking yourself into a sickbed on my account."

"You can count on me, sir," she promised, with

a wry glance. "I'm much too afraid of your cooking to ever be at the mercy of it."

He started to say something, turned, and went out the door.

Jennifer spent the rest of the day finishing up the typing. Then she swept and dusted and made supper—a ham-and-egg casserole, biscuits, and cabbage. Supper sat on the table, however, and began to congeal. Eventually, she warmed up a little of it for herself, ate it, put the rest in the refrigerator, and went to bed. She had a feeling it was an omen for the future. He'd mentioned something that first day about rarely being home before bedtime. But couldn't he have warned her at lunch?

She woke up on time her second morning at the ranch. By 6:15 she was moving gracefully around the spacious kitchen in jeans and a green tee shirt. Apparently, Everett didn't mind what she wore, so she might as well be comfortable. She cooked a huge breakfast of fresh sausage, eggs, and biscuits, and made a pot of coffee.

Everything was piping hot and on the table when Everett came into the kitchen in nothing but his undershorts. Barefooted and bare-chested, he was enough to hold any woman's eyes. Jennifer, who'd seen her share of almost-bare men on the beaches, stood against the counter and stared like a star-struck girl. There wasn't an ounce of fat anywhere on that big body, and he was covered with thick black hair—all over his chest, his flat stomach, his broad thighs. He was as sensuously male as any leading man on television, and she couldn't drag her fascinated eyes away.

He cocked an eyebrow at her, his eyes faintly amused at what he recognized as shocked fascination. "I thought I heard something moving around down here. It's just as well I took time to climb into my shorts." And he turned away to leave her standing there, gaping after him.

A minute later he was back, whipping a belt around the faded blue denims he'd stepped into. He was still barefooted and bare-chested as he sat down at the table across from her.

"I thought I told you to stay in bed," he said as he reached for a biscuit.

"I was afraid you'd keel over out on the plains and your horse wouldn't be able to toss you onto his back and bring you home." She grinned at his puzzled expression. "Well, that's what Texas horses do in western movies."

He chuckled. "Not my horse. He's barely smart enough to find the barn when he's hungry." He buttered the biscuit. "My aunt used to cook like this," he remarked. "Biscuits as light as air."

"Sometimes they bounce," she warned him. "I got lucky."

He gave her a wary glance. "If these biscuits are any indication, so did I," he murmured.

"I saw a henhouse out back. Do I gather the eggs every day?"

"Yes, but watch where you put your hand," he cautioned. "Snakes have been known to get in there."

She shuddered delicately, nodding.

They ate in silence for several minutes before he spoke again. "You're a good cook, Jenny."

She grinned. "My mother taught me. She was terrific."

"Are your parents still alive?"

She shook her head, feeling a twinge of nostalgia. "No. They died several months ago, in a plane crash."

"I'm sorry. Were you close?"

"Very." She glanced at him. "Are your parents dead?"

His face closed up. "Yes," he said curtly, and in a tone that didn't encourage further questions.

She looked up again, her eyes involuntarily lingering on his bare chest. She felt his gaze, and abruptly averted her own eyes back to her empty plate.

He got up after a minute and went back to his bedroom. When he came out, he was tucking in a buttoned khaki shirt, and wearing boots as well. "Thanks for breakfast," he said. "Now, how about taking it easy for the rest of the day? I want to be sure you're up to housework before you pitch in with both hands."

"I won't do anything I'm not able to do," she promised.

"I've got some rope in the barn," he said with soft menace, while his eyes measured her for it.

She stared at him thoughtfully. "I'll be sure to carry a pair of scissors on me."

He was trying not to grin. "My God, you're stubborn."

"Look who's talking."

"I've had lots of practice working cattle," he replied. He picked up his coffee cup and drained it. "From now on, I'll come to the table dressed. Even at six o'clock in the morning."

She looked up, smiling. "You're a nice man, Mr. Culhane," she said. "I'm not a prude, honestly I'm not. It's just that I'm not accustomed to sitting down to breakfast with men. Dressed or undressed."

His dark eyes studies her. "Not liberated, Miss King?" he asked.

She sensed a deeper intent behind that question, but she took it at face value. "I was never unliberated. I'm just old-fashioned."

"So am I, honey. You stick to your guns." He reached for his hat and walked off, whistling.

She was never sure quite how to take what he said. As the days went by, he puzzled her more and more. She noticed him watching her occasionally, when he was in the house and not working with his cattle. But it wasn't a leering kind of look. It was faintly curious and a little protective. She had the odd feeling that he didn't think of her as a woman at all. Not that she found the thought surprising.

Her mirror gave her inescapable proof that she had little to attract a man's eye these days. She was still frail and washed out.

Eddie was the elder of the ranchhands, and Jenny liked him on sight. He was a lot like the boss. He hardly ever smiled, he worked like two men, and he almost never sat down. But Jenny coaxed him into the kitchen with a cold glass of tea at the end of the week, when he brought her the eggs before she could go looking for them.

"Thank you, ma'am. I can sure use this." He sighed, and drained almost the whole glass in a few swallows. "Boss had me fixing fence. Nothing I hate worse than fixing fence," he added with a hard stare.

She tried not to grin. With his jutting chin and short graying whiskers and half-bald head, he did look fierce.

"I appreciate your bringing in the eggs for me," she replied. "I got busy mending curtains and forgot about them."

He shrugged. "It wasn't much," he murmured. He narrowed one eye as he studied her. "You ain't the kind I'd expect the boss to hire."

Her eyebrows arched and she did grin this time. "What would you expect?"

He cleared his throat. "Well, the boss being the way he is . . . an older lady with a mean temper." He moved restlessly in the chair he was straddling. "Well, it takes a mean temper to deal with him. I know, I been doin' it for nigh on twenty years."

"Has he owned the Circle C for that long?" she asked.

"He ain't old enough," he reminded her. "I mean, I knowed him that long. He used to hang around here with his Uncle Ben when he was just a tadpole. His parents never had much use for him. His mama run off with some man when he was ten and his daddy drank hisself to death."

It was like having the pins knocked out from under her. She could imagine Everett at ten, with no mother and an alcoholic father. Her eyes mirrored the horror she felt. "His brother must have been just a baby," she burst out.

"He was. Old Ben and Miss Emma took him in. But Everett weren't so lucky. He had to stay with his daddy."

She studied him quietly, and filled the tea glass again. "Why doesn't he like city women?"

"He got mixed up with some social-climbing lady from Houston," he said curtly. "Anybody could have seen she wouldn't fit in here, except Everett. He'd just inherited the place and had these big dreams of making a fortune in cattle. The fool woman listened to the dreams and came harking out here with him one summer." He laughed bitterly. "Took her all of five minutes to give Everett back his ring and tell him what she thought of his plans. Everett got drunk that night, first time I ever knew him to take a drink of anything stronger than beer. And that was the last time he brought a woman here. Until you come along, at least."

She sat back down, all too aware of the faded yellow shirt and casual jeans she was wearing. The shirt was Everett's. She'd borrowed it while she washed her own in the ancient chugging washing machine. "Don't look at me like a contender," she laughed, tossing back her long dark-blond hair. "I'm just a hanger-on myself, not a chic city woman."

"For a hanger-on," he observed, indicating the scrubbed floors and clean, pressed curtains at the windows and the food cooking on the stove, "you do get through a power of work."

"I like housework," she told him. She sipped her own tea. "I used to fix up houses for a living, until it got too much for me. I got frail during the winter and I haven't quite picked back up yet."

"That accent of yours throws me," he muttered. "Sounds like a lot of Southern mixed up with Yankee."

She laughed again. "I'm from Georgia. Smart man, aren't you?"

"Not so smart, lady, or I'd be rich, too," he said with a rare grin. He got up. "Well, I better get back to work. The boss don't hold with us lollygagging on his time, and Bib's waiting for me to help him move cattle."

"Thanks again for bringing my eggs," she said.

He nodded. "No trouble."

She watched him go, sipping her own tea. There were a lot of things about Everett Culhane that were beginning to make sense. She felt that she understood him a lot better now, right down to the black moods that made him walk around brooding sometimes in the evening.

It was just after dark when Everett came in, and Jenny put the cornbread in the oven to warm the minute she heard the old pickup coming up the driveway. She'd learned that Everett Culhane didn't work banker's hours. He went out at dawn and might not come home until bedtime. But he had yet to find himself without a meal. Jenny prided herself in keeping not only his office, but his home, in order.

He tugged off his hat as he came in the back door. He looked even more weary than usual, covered in dust, his eyes dark-shadowed, his face needing a shave.

She glanced up from the pot of chili she was just taking off the stove and smiled. "Hi, boss. How about some chili and Mexican cornbread?"

"I'm hungry enough to even eat one of those damned salads," he said, glancing toward the stove. He was still wearing his chaps and the leather had a fine layer of dust over it. So did his arms and his dark face.

"If you'll sit down, I'll feed you."

"I need a bath first, honey," he remarked.

"You could rinse off your face and hands in the sink," she suggested, gesturing toward it. "There's a hand towel there, and some soap. You look like you might go to sleep in the shower."

He lifted an eyebrow. "I can just see you pulling me out."

She turned away. "I'd call Eddie or Bib."

"And if you couldn't find them?" he persisted, shedding the chaps on the floor.

"In that case," she said dryly, "I reckon you'd drown, tall man."

"Sassy lady," he accused. He moved behind her and suddenly caught her by the waist with his lean, dark hands. He held her in front of him while he bent over her shoulder to smell the chili. She tried to breathe normally and failed. He was warm and strong at her back, and he smelled of the whole outdoors. She wanted to reach up and kiss that hard, masculine face, and her heart leaped at the uncharacteristic longing.

"What did you put in there?" he asked.

"One armadillo, two rattlers, a quart of beans, some tomatoes, and a hatful of jalapeno peppers."

His hands contracted, making her jump. "A hatful of jalapeno peppers would take the rust off my truck."

"Probably the tires, too," she commented, trying to keep her voice steady. "But Bib told me you Texans like your chili hot."

He turned her around to face him. He searched her eyes for a long, taut moment, and she felt her feet melting into the floor as she looked back. Something seemed to link them for that tiny space of time, joining them soul to soul for one explosive second. She heard him catch his breath and then she was free, all too soon.

"Would . . . would you like a glass of milk with this?" she asked after she'd served the chili into bowls and put it on the table, along with the sliced cornbread and some canned fruit.

"Didn't you make coffee?" he asked, glancing up.

"Sure. I just thought . . ."

"I don't need anything to put out the fire," he told her with a wicked smile. "I'm not a tenderfoot from *Jawja.*"

She moved to the coffeepot and poured two cups. She set his in front of him and sat down. "For your information, suh," she drawled, "we Georgians have been known to eat rattlesnakes while they were still wiggling. And an aunt of mine makes a barbecued sparerib dish that makes Texas chili taste like oatmeal by comparison."

"Is that so? Let's see." He dipped into his chili, savored it, put the spoon down, and glared at her. "You call this hot?" he asked.

She tasted hers and went into coughing spasms. While she was fanning her mouth wildly, he got up with a weary sigh, went to the cupboard, got a glass, and filled it with cold milk.

He handed it to her and sat back down, with a bottle of Tabasco sauce in his free hand. While she gulped milk, he poured half the contents of the bottle into his chili and then tasted it again.

"Just right." He grinned. "But next time, honey, it wouldn't hurt to add another handful of those peppers."

She made a sound between a moan and a gasp and drained the milk glass.

"Now, what were you saying about barbecued spareribs making chili taste like oatmeal?" he asked politely. "I especially liked the part about the rattlers . . ."

"Would you pass the cornbread, please?" she asked proudly.

"Don't you want the rest of your chili?" he returned.

"I'll eat it later," she said. "I made an apple pie for dessert."

He stifled a smile as he dug into his own chili. It got bigger when she shifted her chair so that she didn't have to watch him eat it.

Chapter Four

It had been a long time since Jennifer had been on a horse, but once Everett decided that she was going riding with him one morning, it was useless to argue.

"I'll fall off," she grumbled as she stared up at the palomino gelding he'd chosen for her. "Besides, I've got work to do."

"You've ironed every curtain in the house, washed everything that isn't tied down, scrubbed all the floors, and finished my paperwork. What's left?" he asked, hands low on his hips, his eyes mocking.

"I haven't started supper," she said victoriously.

"So we'll eat late," he replied. "Now, get on."

With a hard glare, she let him put her into the

saddle. She was still weak, but her hair had begun
to regain its earlier luster and her spirit was return-
ing with a vengeance.

"Were you always so domineering, or did you
take lessons?" she asked.

"It sort of comes naturally out here, honey," he
told her with a hard laugh. "You either get tough or
you go broke."

His eyes ran over her, from her short-sleeved
button-up blue print blouse down the legs of her
worn jeans, and he frowned. "You could use some
more clothes," he observed.

"I used to have a closetful," she sighed. "But in
recent months my clothing budget has been pretty
small. Anyway, I don't need to dress up around
here, do I?"

"You could use a pair of new jeans, at least," he
said. His lean hand slid along her thigh gently,
where the material was almost see-through, and
the touch quickened her pulse.

"Yours aren't much better," she protested,
glancing down from his denim shirt to the jeans
that outlined his powerful legs.

"I wear mine out fast," he reminded her.
"Ranching is tough on clothes."

She knew that, having had to get four layers of
mud off his several times. "Well, I don't put mine
to the same use. I don't fix fence and pull calves
and vet cattle."

He lifted an eyebrow. His hand was still resting

absently on her thin leg. "You work hard enough. If I didn't already know it, I'd be told twice a day by Eddie or Bib."

"I like your men." she said.

"They like you. So do I," he added on a smile. "You brighten up the place."

But not as a woman, she thought, watching him. He was completely unaware of her sexually. Even when his eyes did wander over her, it was in an indifferent way. It disturbed her, oddly enough, that he didn't see her as a woman. Because she sure did see him as a man. That sensuous physique was playing on her nerves even now as she glanced down at it with helpless appreciation.

"All we need is a violin," she murmured, grinning.

He stared up at her, but he didn't smile. "Your hair seems lighter," he remarked.

The oddest kind of pleasure swept through her. He'd noticed. She'd just washed it, and the dullness was leaving it. It shimmered with silvery lights where it peeked out from under her hat.

"I just washed it," she remarked.

He shook his head. "It never looked that way before."

"I wasn't healthy before," she returned. "I feel so much better out here," she remarked, sighing as she looked around, with happiness shining out of her like a beacon. "Oh, what a marvelous view! Poor city people."

He turned away and mounted his buckskin gelding. "Come on. I'll show you the bottoms. That's where I've got my new stock."

"Does it flood when it rains?" she asked. It was hard getting into the rhythm of the horse, but somehow she managed it.

"Yes, ma'am, it does," he assured her in a grim tone. "Uncle Ben lost thirty head in a flood when I was a boy. I watched them wash away. Incredible, the force of water when it's unleashed."

"It used to flood back home sometimes," she observed.

"Yes, but not like it does out here," he commented. "Wait until you've seen a Texas rainstorm, and you'll know what I mean."

"I grew up reading Zane Grey," she informed him. "I know all about dry washes and flash floods and stampeding."

"Zane Grey?" he asked, staring at her. "Well, I'll be."

"I told you I loved Texas," she said with a quick smile. She closed her eyes, letting the horse pick its own way beside his. "Just breathe that air," she said lazily. "Rett, I'll bet if you bottled it, you could get rich overnight!"

"I could get rich overnight by selling off oil leases if I wanted to," he said curtly. He lit a cigarette, without looking at her.

She felt as if she'd offended him. "Sorry," she murmured. "Did I hit a nerve?"

"A raw one," he agreed, glancing at her. "Bobby was forever after me about those leases."

"He never won," she said, grinning. "Did he?"

His broad shoulders shifted. "I thought about it once or twice, when times got hard. But it's like a cop-out. I want to make this place pay with cattle, not oil. I don't want my land tied up in oil rigs and pumps cluttering up my landscape." He gestured toward the horizon. "Not too far out there, Apaches used to camp. Santa Ana's troops cut through part of this property on their way to the Alamo. After that, the local cattlemen pooled their cattle here to start them up the Chisolm Trail. During the Civil War, Confederates passed through on their way to Mexico. There's one hell of a lot of history here, and I don't want to spoil it."

She was watching him while he spoke, and her eyes involuntarily lingered on his strong jaw, his sensuous mouth. "Yes," she said softly, "I can understand that."

He glanced at her over his cigarette and smiled. "Where did you grow up?" he asked curiously.

"In a small town in south Georgia," she recalled. "Edison, by name. It wasn't a big place, but it had a big heart. Open fields and lots of pines and a flat horizon like this out beyond it. It's mostly agricultural land there, with huge farms. My grandfather's was very small. Back in his day, it was cotton. Now it's peanuts and soybeans."

"How long did you live there?"

"Until I was around ten," she recalled. "Dad got a job in Atlanta, and we moved there. We lived better, but I never liked it as much as home."

"What did your father do?"

"He was an architect," she said, smiling. "A very good one, too. He added a lot to the city's skyline in his day." She glanced at him. "Your father . . ."

"I don't discuss him," he said matter-of-factly, with a level stare.

"Why?"

He drew in an impatient breath and reined in his horse to light another cigarette. He was chain smoking, something he rarely did. "I said, I don't discuss him."

"Sorry, boss," she replied, pulling her hat down over her eyes in an excellent imitation of tall, lean Bib as she mimicked his drawl. "I shore didn't mean to rile you."

His lips tugged up. He blew out a cloud of smoke and flexed his broad shoulders, rippling the fabric that covered them. "My father was an alcoholic, Jenny."

She knew that already, but she wasn't about to give Eddie away. Everett wouldn't like being gossiped about by his employees. "It must have been a rough childhood for you and Robert," she said innocently.

"Bobby was raised by Uncle Ben and Aunt Emma," he said. "Bobby and I inherited this place from them. They were fine people. Ben spent his life fighting to hold this property. It was a struggle for him to pay taxes. I helped him get into breeding Herefords when I moved in with them. I was just a green kid," he recalled, "all big ears and feet and gigantic ideas. Fifteen, and I had all the answers." He sighed, blowing out another cloud of smoke. "Now I'm almost thirty-five, and every day I come up short of new answers."

"Don't we all?" Jennifer said with a smile. "I was lucky, I suppose. My parents loved each other, and me, and we were well-off. I didn't appreciate it at the time. When I lost them, it was a staggering blow." She leaned forward in the saddle to gaze at the horizon. "How about your mother?"

"A desperate woman, completely undomesticated," he said quietly. "She ran off with the first man who offered her an alternative to starvation. An insurance salesman," he scoffed. "Bobby was just a baby. She walked out the door and never looked back."

"I can't imagine a woman that callous," she said, glancing at him. "Do you ever hear from her now? Is she still alive?"

"I don't know. I don't care." He lifted the cigarette to his chiseled lips. His eyes cut around to meet hers, and they were cold with memory and pain. "I don't much like women."

She felt the impact of the statement to her toes. She knew why he didn't like women, that was the problem, but she was too intelligent to think that she could pry that far, to mention the city woman who'd dumped him because he was poor.

"It would have left scars, I imagine," she agreed.

"Let's ride." He stuck the cigarette between his lips and urged his mount into a gallop.

Riding beside him without difficulty now, Jennifer felt alive and vital. He was such a devastating man, she thought, glancing at him, so sensuous even in faded jeans and shirt. He was powerfully built, like an athlete, and she didn't imagine many men could compete with him.

"Have you ever ridden in rodeo competition?" she asked suddenly without meaning to.

He glanced at her and slowed his mount. "Have I what?"

"Ridden in rodeos?"

He chuckled. "What brought that on?"

"You're so big . . ."

He stopped his horse and stared at her, his wrists crossed over the pommel of his saddle. "Too big," he returned. "The best riders are lean and wiry."

"Oh."

"But in my younger days, I did some bareback riding and bulldogging. It was fun until I broke my arm in two places."

"I'll bet that slowed you down," she murmured dryly.

"It's about the only thing that ever did." He glanced at her rapt face. Live oaks and feathery mesquite trees and prickly pear cactus and wildflowers filled the long space to the horizon and Jennifer was staring at the landscape as if she'd landed in heaven. There were fences everywhere, enclosing pastures where Everett's white-faced Herefords grazed. The fences were old, graying and knotty and more like posts than neatly cut wood, with barbed wire stretched between them.

"Like what you see?" Everett mused.

"Oh, yes," she sighed. "I can almost see it the way it would have been a hundred and more years ago, when settlers and drovers and cattlemen and gunfighters came through here." She glanced at him. "Did you know that Dr. John Henry Holliday, better known as Doc, hailed from Valdosta, Georgia?" she added. "Or that he went west because the doctors said he'd die of tuberculosis if he didn't find a drier climate quick? Or that he and his cousin were supposed to be married, and when they found out about the TB, he went west and she joined a nunnery in Atlanta? And that he once backed down a gang of cowboys in Dodge City and saved Wyatt Earp's life?"

He burst out laughing. "My God, you do know your history, don't you?"

"There was this fantastic biography of Holliday by John Myers Myers," she told him. "It was the most exciting book I ever read. I wish I had a copy. I tried to get one once, but it was out of print."

"Isn't Holliday buried out West somewhere?" he asked.

"In Glenwood Springs, Colorado," she volunteered. "He had a standing bet that a bullet would get him before the TB did, but he lost. He died in a sanitarium out there. He always said he had the

edge in gunfights, because he didn't care if he
died—and most men did." She smiled. "He was a
frail little man, not at all the way he's portrayed in
films most of the time. He was blond and blue-eyed
and most likely had a slow Southern drawl. Gun-
fighter, gambler, and heavy drinker he might have
been, but he had some fine qualities, too, like
loyalty and courage."

"We had a few brave men in Texas, too," he
said, smoking his cigarette with a grin. "Some of
them fought a little battle with a few thousand
Mexicans in a Spanish mission in San Antonio."

"Yes, in the Alamo," she said, grinning. "In
1836, and some of those men were from Georgia."

He burst out laughing. "I can't catch you out on
anything, can I?"

"I'm proud of my state," she told him. "Even
though Texas does feel like home, too. If my
grandfather hadn't come back, I might have been
born here."

"Why did he go back?" he asked, curious.

"I never knew," she said. "But I expect he got
into trouble. He was something of a hell-raiser
even when I knew him." She recalled the little old
man sitting astride a chair in her mother's kitchen,
relating hair-raising escapes from the Germans
during World War I while he smoked his pipe. He'd
died when she was fourteen, and she still remembered going to Edison for the funeral, to a ceme-
tery near Fort Gaines where Spanish moss fell from
the trees. It had been a quiet place, a fitting place

for the old gentleman to be laid to rest. In his home country. Under spreading oak trees.

"You miss him," Everett said quietly.

"Yes."

"My Uncle Ben was something like that," he murmured, lifting his eyes to the horizon. "He had a big heart and a black temper. Sometimes it was hard to see the one for the other," he added with a short laugh. "I idolized him. He had nothing, but he bowed to no man. He'd have approved of what I'm doing with this place. He'd have fought the quick money, too. He liked a challenge."

And so, she would have bet, did his nephew. She couldn't picture Everett Culhane liking anything that came too easily. He would have loved living in the nineteenth century, when a man could build an empire.

"You'd have been right at home here in the middle eighteen hundreds," she remarked, putting the thought into words. "Like John Chisum, you'd have built an empire of your own."

"Think so?" he mused. He glanced at her. "What do you think I'm trying to do now?"

"The same thing," she murmured. "And I'd bet you'll succeed."

He looked her over. "Would you?" His eyes caught hers and held them for a long moment before he tossed his cigarette onto the ground and stepped down out of the saddle to grind it under his boot.

A sudden sizzling sound nearby shocked Jennifer, but it did something far worse to the horse she was riding. The gelding suddenly reared up, and when it came back down again it was running wild.

She pulled back feverishly on the reins, but the horse wouldn't break its speed at all. "Whoa!" she yelled into its ear. "Whoa, you stupid animal!"

Finally, she leaned forward and hung on to the reins and the horse's mane at the same time, holding on with her knees as well. It was a wild ride, and she didn't have time to worry about whether or not she was going to survive it. In the back of her mind she recalled Everett's sudden shout, but nothing registered after that.

The wind bit into her face, her hair came loose from its neat bun. She closed her eyes and began to pray. The jolting pressure was hurting, actually jarring her bones. If only she could keep from falling off!

She heard a second horse gaining on them, then, and she knew that everything would be all right. All she had to do was hold on until Everett could get to her.

But at that moment, the runaway gelding came to a fence and suddenly began to slow down. He balked at the fence, but Jennifer didn't. She sailed right over the animal's head to land roughly on her back in the pasture on the other side of the barbed wire.

The breath was completely knocked out of her. She lay there staring up at leaves and blue sky, feeling as if she'd never get a lungful of air again.

Nearby, Everett was cursing steadily, using words she'd never heard before, even from angry clients back in New York City. She saw his face come slowly into focus above her and was fascinated by its paleness. His eyes were colorful enough, though, like brown flames glittering at her.

"Not . . . my . . . fault," she managed to protest in a thin voice.

"I know that," he growled. "It was mine. Damned rattler, and me without my gun . . ."

"It didn't . . . bite you?" she asked apprehensively, her eyes widening with fear.

He blew out a short breath and chuckled. "No, it didn't. Sweet Jenny. Half dead in a fall, and you're worried about me. You're one in a million, honey."

He bent down beside her. "Hurt anywhere?" he asked gently.

"All over," she said. "Can't get . . . my breath."

"I'm not surprised. Damned horse. We'll put him in your next batch of chili, I promise," he said on a faint smile. "Let's see how much damage you did."

His lean, hard hands ran up and down her legs and arms, feeling for breaks. "How about your back?" he asked, busy with his task.

"Can't . . . feel it yet."

"You will," he promised ruefully.

She was still just trying to breathe. She'd heard of people having the breath knocked out of them, but never knew what it was until now. Her eyes searched Everett's quietly.

"Am I dead?" she asked politely.

"Not quite." He brushed the hair away from her cheeks. "Feel like sitting up?"

"If you'll give me a hand, I'll try," she said huskily.

He raised her up and that was when she noticed that her blouse had lost several buttons, leaving her chest quite exposed. And today of all days she hadn't worn a bra.

Her hands went protectively to the white curves of her breasts, which were barely covered.

"None of that," he chided. "We don't have that kind of relationship. I'm not going to embarrass you by staring. Now get up."

That was almost the final blow. Even half dressed, he still couldn't accept her as a woman. She wanted to sit down on the grass and bawl. It wouldn't have done any good, but it might have eased the sudden ache in her heart.

She let him help her to her feet and staggered unsteadily on them. Her pale eyes glanced toward the gelding, now happily grazing in the pasture across the fence.

"First," she sputtered, "I'm going to dig a deep pit. Then I'm going to fill it with six-foot rattlesnakes. Then I'm going to get a backhoe and shove that stupid horse in there!"

"Wouldn't you rather eat him?" he offered.

"On second thought, I'll gain weight," she muttered. "Lots of it. And I'll ride him two hours every morning."

"You could use a few pounds," he observed, studying her thinness. "You're almost frail."

"I'm not," she argued. "I'm just puny, remember? I'll get better."

"I guess you already have," he murmured dryly. "You sure do get through the housework."

"Slowly but surely," she agreed. She tugged her blouse together and tied the bottom edges together.

When she looked back up, his eyes were watching her hands with a strange, intent stare. He looked up and met her puzzled gaze.

"Are you okay now?" he asked.

"Just a little shaky," she murmured with a slight grin.

"Come here." He bent and lifted her easily into his arms, shifting her weight as he turned, and walked toward the nearby gate in the fence.

She was shocked by her reaction to being carried by him. She felt ripples of pleasure washing over her body like fire, burning where his chest touched her soft breasts. Even through two layers of fabric, the contact was wildly arousing, exciting. She clamped her teeth together hard to keep from giving in to the urge to grind her body against his. He was a man, after all, and not invulnerable. She could start something that she couldn't stop.

"I'm too heavy," she protested once.

"No," he said gently, glancing down into her eyes unsmilingly. "You're like feathers. Much too light."

"Most women would seem light to you," she murmured, lowering her eyes to his shirt. Where the top buttons were undone, she saw the white of his tee shirt and the curl of dark, thick hair. He smelled of leather and wind and tobacco and she wanted so desperately to curl up next to him and kiss that hard, chiseled mouth . . .

"Open the gate," he said, nodding toward the latch.

She reached out and unfastened it, and pushed until it came free of the post. He went through and let her fasten it again. When she finished, she noticed that his gaze had fallen to her body. She followed it, embarrassed to find that the edges of her blouse gapped so much, that one creamy pink breast was completely bare to his eyes.

Her hand went slowly to the fabric, tugging it into place. "Sorry," she whispered self-consciously.

"So am I. I didn't mean to stare," he said quietly, shifting her closer to his chest. "Don't be embarrassed, Jenny."

She drew in a slow breath, burying her red face in his throat. He stiffened before he drew her even closer, his arms tautening until she was crushed to his broad, warm chest.

He didn't say a word as he walked, and neither did she. But she could feel the hard beat of his heart, the ragged sigh of his breath, the stiffening of his body against her taut breasts. In ways she'd never expected, her body sang to her, exquisite songs of unknown pleasure, of soft touches and wild contact. Her hands clung to Everett's neck, her eyes closed. She wanted this to last forever.

All too soon, they reached the horses. Everett let her slide down his body in a much too arousing way, so that she could feel the impact of every single inch of him on the way to the ground. And then, his arms contracted, holding her, bringing her into the length of him, while his cheek rested on her hair and the wind blew softly around them.

She clung, feeling the muscles of his back tense under her hands, loving the strength and warmth and scent of him. She'd never wanted anything so much as she wanted this closeness. It was sweet and heady and satisfying in a wild new way.

Seconds later, he let her go, just as she imagined she felt a fine tremor in his arms.

"Are you all right?" he asked softly.

"Yes," she said, trying to smile, but she couldn't look up at him. It had been intimate, that embrace. As intimate as a kiss in some ways, and it had caused an unexpected shift in their relationship.

"We'd better get back," he said. "I've got work to do."

"So have I," she said quickly, mounting the

gelding with more apprehension than courage. "All right, you ugly horse," she told it. "You do that to me again, and I'll back the pickup truck over you!"

The horse's ears perked up and it moved its head slightly to one side. She burst into laughter. "See, Rett, he heard me!"

But Everett wasn't looking her way. He'd already turned his mount and was smoking another cigarette. And all the way back to the house, he didn't say a word.

As they reached the yard she felt uncomfortably tense. To break the silence, she broached a subject she'd had on her mind all day.

"Rett, could I have a bucket of paint?"

He stared at her. "What?"

"Can I have a bucket of paint?" she asked. "Just one. I want to paint the kitchen."

"Now, look, lady," he said, "I hired you to cook and do housework and type." His eyes narrowed and she fought not to let her fallen spirits show. "I like my house the way it is, with no changes."

"Just one little bucket of paint," she murmured.

"No."

She glared at him, but he glared back just as hard. "If you want to spend money," he said curtly, "I'll buy you a new pair of jeans. But we aren't throwing money away on decorating." He made the word sound insulting.

"Decorating is an art," she returned, defending

her professional integrity. She was about to tell him what she'd done for a living, but as she opened her mouth, he was speaking again.

"It's a high-class con game," he returned hotly. "And even if I had the money, I wouldn't turn one of those fools loose on my house. Imagine paying out good money to let some tasteless idiot wreck your home and charge you a fortune to do it!" He leaned forward in the saddle with a belligerent stare. "No paint. Do we understand each other, Miss King?"

Do we ever, she thought furiously. Her head lifted. "You'd be lucky to get a real decorator in here, anyway," she flung back. "One who wouldn't faint at the way you combine beautiful old oriental rugs with ashtrays made of old dead rattlesnakes!"

His dark eyes glittered dangerously. "It's my house," he said coldly.

"Thank God!" she threw back.

"If you don't like it, close your eyes!" he said. "Or pack your damned bag and go back to Atlanta and turn your nose up . . ."

"I'm not turning my nose up!" she shouted. "I just wanted a bucket of paint!"

"You know when you'll get it, too, don't you?" he taunted. He tipped his hat and rode off, leaving her fuming on the steps.

Yes, she knew. His eyes had told her, graphically. When hell froze over. She remembered in the back of her mind that there was a place called Hell, and once it did freeze over and made national headlines. She only wished she'd saved the newspaper clipping. She'd shove it under his arrogant nose, and maybe then she'd get her paint!

She turned to go into the house, stunned to find Eddie coming out the front door.

He looked red-faced, but he doffed his hat. "Mornin', ma'am," he murmured. "I was just putting the mail on the table."

"Thanks, Eddie," she said with a wan smile.

He stared at her. "Boss lost his temper, I see."

"Yep," she agreed.

"Been a number of days before when he's done that."

"Yep."

"You going to keep it all to yourself, too, ain't you?"

"Yep."

He chuckled, tipped his hat, and went on down the steps. She walked into the house and burst out laughing. She was getting the hang of speaking Texan at last.

Chapter Five

Jennifer spent the rest of the day feverishly washing down the kitchen walls. So decorators were con artists, were they? And he wouldn't turn one loose in his home, huh? She was so enraged that the mammoth job took hardly any time at all. Fortunately, the walls had been done with oil-based paint, so the dirt and grease came off without taking the paint along with them. When she was through, she stood back, worn out and damp with sweat, to survey her handiwork. She had the fan going full blast, but it was still hot and sticky, and she felt the same way herself. The pale yellow walls looked new, making the effort worthwhile.

Now, she thought wistfully, if she only had a few dollars' worth of fabric and some thread, and the use of the aging sewing machine upstairs, she could make curtains for the windows. She could even buy that out of her own pocket, and the interior-decorator-hating Mr. Everett Donald Culhane could just keep his nasty opinions to himself. She laughed, wondering what he'd have said if she'd used his full name while they were riding. Bib had told her his middle name. She wondered if anyone ever called him Donald.

She fixed a light supper of creamed beef and broccoli, remembering that he'd told her he hated both of those dishes. She deliberately made weak coffee. Then she sat down in the kitchen and pared apples while she waited for him to come home. Con artist, huh?

It was getting dark when he walked in the door. He was muddy and tired-looking, and in his lean, dark hand was a small bouquet of slightly wilted wildflowers.

"Here," he said gruffly, tossing them onto the kitchen table beside her coffee cup. The mad profusion of bluebonnets and Indian paintbrush and Mexican hat made blue and orange and red swirls of color on the white tablecloth. "And you can have your damned bucket of paint."

He strode past her toward the staircase, his face hard and unyielding, without looking back. She burst into tears, her fingers trembling as they touched the unexpected gift.

Never in her life had she moved so fast. She dried her tears and ran to pour out the pot of weak coffee. She put on a pot of strong, black coffee and dragged out bacon and eggs and flour, then put the broccoli and chipped beef, covered, into the refrigerator.

By the time Everett came back down, showered and in clean denims, she had bacon and eggs and biscuits on the table.

"I thought you might like something fresh and hot for supper," she said quickly.

He glanced at her as he sat down. "I'm surprised. I was expecting liver and onions or broccoli tonight."

She flushed and turned her back. "Were you? How strange." She got the coffeepot and calmly filled his cup and her own. "Thank you for my flowers," she said without looking at him.

"Don't start getting ideas, Miss King," he said curtly, reaching for a biscuit. "Just because I backed down on the paint, don't expect it to become a habit around here."

She lowered her eyes demurely to the platter of eggs she was dishing up. "Oh, no, sir," she said.

He glanced around the room and his eyes darkened, glittered. They came back to her. He laid down his knife. "Did you go ahead and buy paint?" he asked in a softly menacing tone.

"No, I did not," she replied curtly. "I washed down the walls."

He blinked. "Washed down the walls?" He looked around again, scowling. "In this heat?!"

"Look good, don't they?" she asked fiercely,

smiling. "I don't need the paint, but thank you anyway."

He picked up his fork, lifting a mouthful of eggs slowly to his mouth. He finished his supper before he spoke again. "Why did it matter so much about the walls?" he asked. "The house is old. It needs thousands of dollars' worth of things I can't afford to have done. Painting one room is only going to make the others look worse."

She shrugged. "Old habits," she murmured with a faint smile. "I've been fixing up houses for a long time."

That went right past him. He looked preoccupied. Dark and brooding.

"Is something wrong?" she asked suddenly.

He sighed and pulled an envelope from his pocket and tossed it onto the table. "I found that on the hall table on my way upstairs."

She frowned. "What is it?"

"A notice that the first payment is due on the note I signed at the bank for my new bull." He laughed shortly. "I can't meet it. My tractor broke down and I had to use the money for the payment to fix it. Can't plant without the tractor. Can't feed livestock without growing feed. Ironically, I may have to sell the bull to pay back the money."

Her heart went out to him. Here she sat giving him the devil over a bucket of paint, and he was in serious trouble. She felt terrible.

"I ought to be shot," she murmured quietly.

"I'm sorry I made such a fuss about the paint, Rett."

He laughed without humor. "You didn't know. I told you times were hard."

"Yes. But I didn't realize how hard until now." She sipped her coffee. "How much do you need . . . can I ask?" she said softly.

He sighed. "Six hundred dollars." He shook his head. "I thought I could swing it, I really did. I wanted to pay it off fast."

"I've got last week's salary," she said. "I haven't spent any of it. That would help a little. And you could hold back this week's . . ."

He stared into her wide, soft eyes and smiled. "You're quite a girl, Jenny."

"I want to help."

"I know. I appreciate it. But spend your money on yourself. At any rate, honey, it would hardly be a drop in the bucket. I've got a few days to work it out. I'll turn up something."

He got up and left the table and Jennifer stared after him, frowning. Well, she could help. There had to be an interior-design firm in Houston, which was closer than San Antonio or Austin. She'd go into town and offer her services. With any luck at all, they'd be glad of her expert help. She could make enough on one job to buy Everett's blessed bull outright. She was strong enough now to take on the challenge of a single job. And she would!

As luck would have it, the next morning Eddie mentioned that his wife Libby was going to drive into the city to buy a party dress for his daughter. Jennifer hitched a ride with her after Everett went to work.

Libby was a talker, a blond bearcat of a woman with a fine sense of humor. She was good company, and Jennifer took to her immediately.

"I'm so glad Everett's got you to help around the house," she said as they drove up the long highway to Houston. "I offered, but he wouldn't hear of it. Said I had enough to do, what with raising four kids. He even looks better since you've been around. And he doesn't cuss as much." She grinned.

"I was so delighted to have the job," Jennifer sighed, smiling. She brushed back a stray wisp of blond hair. She was wearing her best blue camisole with a simple navy-blue skirt and her polished white sling pumps with a white purse. She looked elegant, and Libby remarked on it.

"Where are you going, all dressed up?" she asked.

"To get a second job," Jennifer confessed. "But you mustn't tell Everett. I want to surprise him."

Libby looked worried. "You're not leaving?"

"Oh, no! Not until he makes me! This is only a temporary thing," she promised.

"Doing what?"

"Decorating."

"That takes a lot of schooling, doesn't it?" Libby asked, frowning.

"Quite a lot. I graduated from interior-design

school in New York," Jennifer explained. "And I worked in the field for two years. My health gave out and I had to give it up for a while." She sighed. "There was so much pressure, you see. So much competition. My nerves got raw and my resistance got low, and I wound up flat on my back in a hospital with pneumonia. I went home to Atlanta to recuperate, got a job with a temporary talent agency, and met Robert Culhane on an assignment. He offered me a job, and I grabbed it. Getting to work in Texas was pretty close to heaven, for me."

Libby shook her head. "Imagine that."

"I was sorry about Robert," Jennifer said quietly. "I only knew him slightly, but I did like him. Everett still broods about it. He doesn't say much, but I know he misses his brother."

"He was forever looking out for Bobby," Libby confirmed. "Protecting him and such. A lot of the time, Bobby didn't appreciate that. And Bobby didn't like living low. He wanted Everett to sell off those oil rights and get rich. Everett wouldn't."

"I don't blame him," Jennifer said. "If it was my land, I'd feel the same way."

Libby looked surprised. "My goodness, another one."

"I don't like strip-mining, either," Jennifer offered. "Or killing baby seals for their fur or polluting the rivers."

Libby burst out laughing. "You and Everett were made for each other. He's just that way himself."

She glanced at Jennifer as the Houston skyline came into view. "Did Bobby tell you what Everett did the day the oil man came out here to make him that offer, after the geologists found what they believe was oil-bearing land?"

"No."

"The little oil man wanted to argue about it, and Everett had just been thrown by a horse he was trying to saddle-break and was in a mean temper. He told the man to cut it off, and he wouldn't. So Everett picked him up," she said, grinning, "carried him out to his car, put him in, and walked away. We haven't seen any oil men at the ranch since."

Jennifer laughed. It sounded like Everett, all right. She sat back, sighing, and wondered how she was going to make him take the money she hoped to earn. Well, that worry could wait in line. First, she had to find a job.

While Libby went into the store, Jennifer found a telephone directory and looked up the addresses of two design shops. The first one was nearby, so she stopped to arrange a time and place to rendez-vous with Libby that afternoon, and walked the two blocks.

She waited for fifteen minutes to see the man who owned the shop. He listened politely, but impatiently, while she gave her background. She mentioned the name of the firm she'd worked with in New York, and saw his assistant's eyebrows jump up. But the manager was obviously not impressed. He told her he was sorry but he was overstaffed already.

Crestfallen, she walked out and called a taxi to take her to the next company. This time, she had better luck. The owner was a woman, a veritable Amazon, thin and dark and personable. She gave Jennifer a cup of coffee, listened to her credentials, and grinned.

"Lucky me," she laughed. "To find you just when I was desperate for one more designer!"

"You mean, you can give me work?" Jennifer burst out, delighted.

"Just this one job, right now, but it could work into a full-time position," she promised.

"Part-time would be great. You see, I already have a job I'd rather not leave," Jennifer replied.

"Perfect. You can do this one in days. It's only one room. I'll give you the address, and you can go and see the lady yourself. Where are you staying?"

"Just north of Victoria," Jennifer said. "In Big Spur."

"How lovely!" the lady said. "The job's in Victoria! No transportation problem?"

She thought of asking Libby, and smiled. "I have a conspirator," she murmured. "I think I can manage." She glanced up. "Can you estimate my commission?"

Her new employer did, and Jennifer grinned. It would be more than enough for Everett to pay off his note. "Okay!"

"The client, Mrs. Whitehall, doesn't mind paying for quality work," came the lilting reply. "And she'll be tickled when she hears the background of her designer. I'll give her a ring now, if you like."

"Would I! Miss . . . Mrs . . . Ms . . . ?"

"Ms. Sally Ward," the owner volunteered. "I'm glad to meet you, Jennifer King. Now, let's get busy."

Libby was overjoyed when she heard what Jennifer was plotting, and volunteered to drive her back and forth to the home she'd be working on. She even agreed to pinch-hit in the house, so that Everett wouldn't know what was going on. It would be risky, but Jennifer felt it would be very much worth the risk.

As it turned out, Mrs. Whitehall was an elderly lady with an unlimited budget and a garage full of cars. She was more than happy to lend one to Jennifer so that she could drive back and forth to Victoria to get fabric and wallcoverings and to make appointments with painters and carpet-layers.

Jennifer made preliminary drawings after an interview with Mrs. Whitehall, who lived on an enormous estate called Casa Verde.

"My son Jason and his wife Amanda used to live with me," Mrs. Whitehall volunteered. "But since their marriage, they've built a house of their own further down the road. They're expecting their first child. Jason wants a boy and Amanda a girl." She grinned. "From the size of her, I'm expecting twins!"

"When is she due?" Jennifer asked.

"Any day," came the answer. "Jason spends part of the time pacing the floor and the other part daring Amanda to lift, move, walk, or breathe hard." She laughed delightedly. "You'd have to know my son, Miss King, to realize how out of character that is for him. Jason was always such a calm person until Amanda got pregnant. I think it's been harder on him than it has on her."

"Have they been married long?"

"Six years," Mrs. Whitehall said. "So happily. They wanted a child very much, but it took a long time for Amanda to become pregnant. It's been all the world to them, this baby." She stared around the room at the fading wallpaper and the worn carpet. "I've just put this room off for so long. Now I don't feel I can wait any longer to have it done. Once the baby comes, I'll have so many other things to think of. What do you suggest, my dear?"

"I have some sketches," Jennifer said, drawing out her portfolio.

Mrs. Whitehall looked over them, sighing. "Just what I wanted. Just exactly what I wanted." She nodded. "Begin whenever you like, Jennifer. I'll find somewhere else to sit while the workmen are busy."

And so it began. Jennifer spent her mornings at Casa Verde, supervising the work. Afternoons she worked at Everett's ranch. And amazingly, she never got caught.

It only took a few days to complete the work.

Luckily, she found workmen who were between jobs and could take on a small project. By the end of the week, it was finished.

"I can't tell you how impressed I am." Mrs. Whitehall sighed as she studied the delightful new decor, done in soft green and white and dark green.

"It will be even lovelier when **the** furniture is delivered tomorrow." Jennifer grinned. "I'm so proud of it. I hope you like it half as much as I do."

"I do, indeed," Mrs. Whitehall said. "I . . ."

The ringing of the phone halted her. She picked up the extension at her side. "Hello?" She sat up straight. "Yes, Jason! When?" She laughed, covering the receiver. "It's a boy!" She moved her hand. "What are you going to name him? Oh, yes, I like that very much. Joshua Brand Whitehall. Yes, I do. How is Amanda? Yes, she's tough, all right. Dear, I'll be there in thirty minutes. Now you calm down, dear. Yes, I know it isn't every day a man has a son. I'll see you soon. Yes, dear."

She hung up. "Jason's beside himself," she said, smiling. "He wanted a boy so much. And they can have others. Amanda will get her girl yet. I must rush."

Jennifer stood up. "Congratulations on that new grandbaby," she said. "And I've enjoyed working with you very much."

"I'll drop you off at the ranch on my way," Mrs. Whitehall offered.

"It's a good little way," Jennifer began, wondering how she'd explain it to Everett. Mrs. Whitehall drove a Mercedes-Benz.

"Nonsense." Mrs. Whitehall laughed. "It's no trouble at all. Anyway, I want to talk to you about doing some more rooms. This is delightful. Very creative. I never enjoyed redecorating before, but you make it exciting."

After that, how could Jennifer refuse? She got in the car.

Luckily enough, Everett wasn't in sight when she reached the ranch. Mrs. Whitehall let her out at the steps and Jennifer rushed inside, nervous and wild-eyed. But the house was empty. She almost collapsed with relief. And best of all, on the hall table was an envelope addressed to her from Houston, from the interior-design agency. She tore it open and found a check and a nice letter offering more work. The check was for the amount Everett needed, plus a little. Jennifer endorsed it, grinning, and went in to fix supper.

Chapter Six

Everett came home just before dark, but he didn't come into the house. Jennifer had a light supper ready, just cold cuts and bread so there wouldn't be anything to reheat. When he didn't appear after she heard the truck stop, she went out to look for him.

He was standing by the fence, staring at the big Hereford bull he'd wanted so badly. Jennifer stood on the porch and watched him, her heart aching for him. She'd decided already to cash her check first thing in the morning and give it to him at breakfast. But she wondered if she should mention it now. He looked so alone . . .

She moved out into the yard, the skirt of her blue shirtwaist dress blowing in the soft, warm breeze.

"Rett?" she called.

He glanced at her briefly. "Waiting supper on me again?" he asked quietly.

"No. I've only made cold cuts." She moved to the fence beside him and stared at the big, burly bull. "He sure is big."

"Yep." He took out a cigarette and lit it, blowing out a cloud of smoke. He looked very western in his worn jeans, batwing chaps, and close-fitting denim shirt, which was open halfway down his chest. He was a sensuous man, and she loved looking at him. Her eyes went up to his hard mouth and she wondered for what seemed the twentieth time how it would feel on her own. That made her burn with embarrassment, and she turned away.

"Suppose I offered you what I've saved?" she asked.

"We've been through all that. No. Thank you," he added. "I can't go deeper in debt, not even to save my bull. I'll just pay off the note and start over. The price of beef is expected to start going up in a few months. I'll stand pat until it does."

"Did anyone ever tell you that you have a double dose of pride?" she asked, exasperated.

He looked down at her, his eyes shadowed in the dusk by the brim of his hat. "Look who's talking about pride, for God's sake," he returned. "Don't I remember that you tried to walk back to town carrying a suitcase and a typewriter in the blazing sun with no hat? I had to threaten to tie you in the truck to get you inside it."

"I knew you didn't want me here," she said simply. "I didn't want to become a nuisance."

"I don't think I can imagine that. You being a nuisance, I mean." He took another draw from the cigarette and crushed it out. "I've had a good offer for the bull from one of my neighbors. He's coming over tomorrow to talk to me about it."

Well, that gave her time to cash the check and make one last effort to convince him, she thought.

"Why are you wearing a dress?" he asked, staring down at her. "Trying to catch my eye, by any chance?"

"Who, me?" she laughed. "As you told me the other day, we don't have that kind of relationship."

"You were holding me pretty hard that day the rattlesnake spooked your horse," he said unexpectedly, and he didn't smile. "And you didn't seem to mind too much that I saw you without your shirt."

She felt the color work its way into her hairline. "I'd better put supper on the . . . oh!"

He caught her before she could move away and brought her gently against the length of his body. His hand snaked around her waist, holding her there, and the other one spread against her throat, arching it.

"Just stand still," he said gently. "And don't start anything. I know damned good and well you're a virgin. I'm not going to try to seduce you."

Her breath was trapped somewhere below her windpipe. She felt her knees go wobbly as she saw the narrowness of his eyes, the hard lines of his face. She'd wanted it so much, but now that it was happening, she was afraid.

She stilled and let her fingers rest over his shirt, but breathing had become difficult. He felt strong and warm and she wanted to touch his hair-roughened skin. It looked so tantalizing to her innocent eyes.

He was breathing slowly, steadily. His thumb nudged her chin up so that he could look into her eyes. "You let me look at you," he said under his breath. "I've gone half mad remembering that, wondering how many other men have seen you that way."

"No one has," she replied quietly. She couldn't drag her eyes from his. She could feel his breath, taste the smokiness of it, smell the leather and tobacco smells of his big, hard body so close to hers. "Only you."

His chest rose heavily. "Only me?"

"I was career-minded," she said hesitantly. "I didn't want commitment, so I didn't get involved. Everett . . ."

"No. I don't want to fight." He took her hands and slid them up and down over the hard muscles of his chest. His breathing changed suddenly.

He bent and drew her lower lip down with the soft pressure of his thumb. He fit his own mouth to it with exquisite patience, opening it slowly, tempting it, until she stood very still and closed her eyes.

His free hand brought her body close against his.

The other one slowly undid the top two buttons of her dress and moved inside to her throat, her shoulder, her collarbone. His mouth increased its ardent pressure as his fingers spread, and his breathing became suddenly ragged as he arched her body and found the soft rise of her breast with his whole hand.

She gasped and instinctively caught his wrist. But he lifted his mouth and looked into her eyes and slowly shook his head. "You're old enough to be taught this," he said quietly. "I know how delicate you are here," he breathed, brushing his fingers over the thin lace. "I'm going to be very gentle, and you're going to enjoy what I do to you. I promise. Close your eyes, honey."

His mouth found hers again, even as he stopped speaking. It moved tenderly on her trembling lips, nibbling, demanding, in a silence bursting with new sensations and promise.

She clung to his shirtfront, shocked to find that her legs were trembling against his, that her breath was coming quick enough to be audible. She tried to pull away, but his fingers slid quietly under the bra and found bare, vulnerable skin, and she moaned aloud.

Her nails bit into his chest. "Rett!" she gasped, on fire with hunger and frightened and embarrassed that he could see and feel her reaction to him.

"Shhhh," he whispered at her mouth, gentling

her. "It's all right. It's all right to let me see. You're so sweet, Jenny Wren. Like a bright new penny without a single fingerprint except mine." His mouth touched her closed eyelids, her forehead. His fingers contracted gently, his palm feeling the exquisite tautening of her body as she clung to him and shuddered. "Yes, you like that, don't you?" he breathed. His mouth brushed her eyelids again, her nose, her mouth. "Jenny, put your hand inside my shirt."

His voice was deep and low and tender. She obeyed him blindly, on fire with reckless hunger, needing to touch and taste and feel him. Her hands slid under his shirt and flattened on hair and warm muscle, and he tautened.

"Does that . . . make you feel the way . . . I feel?" she whispered shakily, looking up at him.

"Exactly," he whispered back. He moved his hand from her breast to her neck and pressed her face slowly against his bare chest.

She seemed to sense what he wanted. Her mouth touched him there tentatively, shyly, and he moaned. He smelled of faint cologne and tobacco, and she liked the way his hard muscles contracted where she touched them with her hands and her lips. He was all man. All man. And her world was suddenly narrowed to her senses, and Everett.

He took her face in his hands and tilted it, bending to kiss her with a hungry ferocity that would have frightened her minutes before. But she

went on tiptoe and linked her arms around his neck
and gave him back the kiss, opening her mouth
under his to incite him to further intimacy, shiver-
ing wildly when he accepted the invitation and his
tongue went into the sweet darkness in a slow,
hungry tasting.

When he finally released her, he was shaking
too. His eyes burned with frustrated desire, his
hands framed her face, hot and hard.

"We have to stop. Now."

She took a slow, steadying breath. "Yes."

He took his hands away and moved toward the
house, lighting a cigarette eventually after two
fumbles.

She followed him, drunk on sensual pleasure,
awed by what she'd felt with him, by what she'd let
him do. She felt shy when they got into the house,
into the light, and she couldn't quite meet his eyes.

"I'll get supper on the table," she said.

He didn't even reply. He followed her into the
kitchen, and with brooding dark eyes watched her
move around.

She poured coffee and he sat down, still watching
her.

Her hand trembled as she put the cream pitcher
beside his cup. He caught her fingers, looking up at
her with a dark, unsmiling stare.

"Don't start getting self-conscious with me," he
said quietly. "I know you've never let another man
touch you like that. I'm proud that you let me."

She stared at him, eyes widening. Of all the things she'd expected he might say, that wasn't one of them.

His nostrils flared and his hand contracted. "After supper," he said slowly, holding her eyes, "I'm going to carry you into the living room and lay you down on the sofa. And I'm going to make love to you, in every way I know. And when I get through, you'll shudder at the thought of another man's hands on you."

His eyes were blazing, and her own kindled. Her lips parted. "Rett, I can't . . . you know."

He nodded. "We won't go that far." His fingers caressed her wrist and his face hardened. "How hungry are you?" he asked under his breath.

Her heart was beating wildly. She looked at him and it was suicide. She felt shaky to her toes.

"Make love to me," she whispered blindly as she reached for him.

He twisted her down across his lap and found her mouth in a single motion. He groaned as he kissed her, his breath sighing out raggedly.

"Oh, God, I need you," he ground out, standing with her in his arms. "I need you so much!"

He turned, still kissing her, and carried her through into the living room, putting her gently down on the worn couch. After giving her a hot stare, he turned and methodically drew all the curtains and closed and locked the door. Then he came back, sitting down so that he was facing her.

"Now," he whispered, bending with trembling

hands to the bodice of her dress. "Now, let's see how much damage we can do to each other's self-control, Jenny Wren. I want to look at you until I ache to my toes!"

He unbuttoned it and she sank back against the pillows, watching unprotestingly. He half lifted her and slipped the dress down her arms. Her bra followed it. And then he leaned over her, just looking at the soft mounds he'd uncovered.

His fingers stroked one perfect breast, lingering on the tip until she cried out.

"Does that hurt?" he whispered, looking into her eyes.

She was trembling, and it was hard to talk. "No," she breathed.

He smiled slowly, in a tender, purely masculine way, and repeated the brushing caress. She arched up, and his eyes blazed like dark fires.

"Jenny!" he growled. His fingers held her breasts up to his hard mouth. He took her by surprise, and she moaned wildly as she felt the warm moistness envelop her. Her hands dug into his hair and she dragged his head closer, whimpering as if she were being tortured.

"Not so hard, baby," he whispered raggedly, lifting his head. "You're too delicate for that, Jenny."

"Rett," she moaned, her eyes wild.

"Like this, then," he whispered, bending to grind his mouth into hers. His hand swallowed her, stroking, molding, and she trembled all over as if with a fever, clinging to him, needing something more than this, something closer, something far, far more intimate. . . .

Her hands moved against his chest, trembling as they explored the hard muscles.

"Be still now," he whispered, easing her back into the cushions. "Don't move under me. Just lie still, Jenny Wren, and let me show you . . . how bodies kiss."

She held her breath as his body moved completely onto hers. She felt the blatant maleness of it, the warmth, the tickle of hair against her soft breasts, the exquisite weight, and her hungry eyes looked straight into his as they joined.

"Oh," she whispered jerkily.

"Sweet, sweet Jenny," he breathed, cupping her face in his hands. "It's like moving on velvet. Do you feel me . . . all of me?"

"Yes." Her own hands went to his back, found their way under his shirt. "Rett, you're very heavy," she said with a shaky smile.

"Too heavy?" he whispered.

"Oh, no," she said softly. "I . . . like the way it feels."

"So do I." He bent and kissed her, tenderly, in a new and delicious way. "Not afraid?"

"No."

"You will be," he whispered softly. His hands moved down, sliding under her hips. He lifted his head and looked down at her just as his fingers contracted and ground her hips up into his in an intimacy that made her gasp and cry out.

He shuddered, and she buried her face in his hot throat, dizzy and drowning in deep water, burning with exquisite sensation and blinding pleasure.

"Jenny," he groaned. His hands hurt. "Jenny, Jenny, if you weren't a virgin, I'd take you. I'd take you, here, now, in every way there is . . . !"

She barely heard him, she was shaking so badly. All at once, he eased himself down beside her and folded her into his arms in a strangely protective way. His hands smoothed her back, his lips brushed over her face in tiny, warm kisses. All the passion was suddenly gone, and he was comforting her.

"I never believed . . . what my mother used to say about . . . passion," Jenny whispered at his ear, still trembling. "Rett, it's exquisite . . . isn't it? So explosive and sweet and dangerous!"

"You've never wanted a man before?" he breathed.

"No."

"I'll tell you something, Jenny. I've never wanted a woman like this. Not ever." He kissed her ear softly. "I want you to know something. If it ever happened, even accidentally, you'd never want to forget it. I'd take you so tenderly, so slowly, that you'd never know anything about pain."

"Yes, I know that," she murmured, smiling. Her

arms tightened. "You could have had me, then, lofty principles and all," she added ruefully. "I didn't realize how easy it was to throw reason to the wind."

"You're a very passionate woman." He lifted his head and searched her eyes. "I didn't expect that."

"You didn't seem much like a passionate man either," she confessed, letting her eyes wander slowly over his hard, dark face. "Oh, Rett, I did want you in the most frightening way!"

His chest expanded roughly. "Jenny, I think we'd better get up from here. My good intentions only seem to last until I get half your clothes off."

She watched him draw away, watched how his eyes clung to her bare breasts, and she smiled and arched gently.

"Oh, God, don't do that!" he whispered, shaken, as he turned away.

She laughed delightedly and sat up, getting back into her clothes as she stared at his broad back. He was smoking a cigarette, running a restless hand through his hair. And he was the handsomest man she'd ever seen in her life. And the most . . . loved.

I love you, she thought dreamily. I love every line and curve and impatient gesture you make. I'd rather live here, in poverty, with you than to have the world in the bank.

"I'm decent now," she murmured, smiling when he turned hesitantly around. "My gosh, you make me feel good. I was always self-conscious about being so small."

His eyes narrowed. "You're not small, baby," he said in a gruff tone. "You're just delicate."

Her face glowed with pride. "Thank you, Rett."

"Let's see if the coffee's still warm," he said softly, holding out his hand.

She took it, and he pulled her up, pausing to bend and kiss her slowly, lingering over the soft, swollen contours of her warm mouth.

"I've bruised your lips," he whispered. "Are they sore?"

"They're delightfully sensitive," she whispered back, going on tiptoe. "You know a lot about kissing for a cattleman."

"You know a lot for a virgin," he murmured, chuckling.

"Pat yourself on the back, I'm a fast study." She slid her hand pertly inside his shirt and stroked him. "See?"

He took her hand away and buttoned his shirt to the throat. "I'm going to have to watch you, lady," he murmured, "or you'll wrestle me down on the couch and seduce me one dark night."

"It's all right," she whispered. "I won't get you pregnant. You can trust me, honey," she added with a wicked smile.

He burst out laughing and led her into the kitchen. "Feed me," he said, "before we get in over our heads."

"Spoilsport. Just when things were getting interesting."

"Another minute, and they'd have gone past interesting to educational," he murmured dryly, with a pointed glance. "Men get hot pretty fast that way, Jenny. Don't rely on my protective instincts too far. I damned near lost my head."

"Did you, really?" she asked, all eyes. "But I don't know anything."

"That's why," he sighed. "I . . . haven't touched a virgin since I was one myself. Funny, isn't it, that these days it's become a stigma. Back when I was a kid, decent boys wouldn't be seen with a girl who had a reputation for being easy. Now it's the virgins who take all the taunting." He stopped, turning her, and his face was solemn. "I'm glad you're still innocent. I'm glad that I can look at you and make you blush, and watch all those first reactions that you've never shown anybody else. To hell with modern morality, Jenny. I love the fact that you're as old-fashioned as I am."

"So do I. Now," she added, studying him warmly. "Rett . . ." Her fingers went up and touched his hard mouth. "Rett, I think I . . ." She was about to say "love you" when a piece of paper on the floor caught his eye.

"Hey, what's this?" he asked, bending to pick it up.

Her heart stopped. It was the check she'd gotten in the mail. She'd stuck it in her pocket, but it must have fallen out. She watched him open it and read the logo at the top with a feeling of impending disaster. She hadn't meant to tell him where it came from just yet. . . .

His lean hand closed around the check, crumpling it. "Where did you get this kind of money, and what for?" he demanded.

"I . . . I worked part-time for a design house in Houston, decorating a lady's living room," she blurted out. "It's for you. To pay off your bull," she said, her face bright, her eyes shining. "I went to Houston and got a part-time job decorating a living room. That's my commission. Surprise! Now you won't have to sell that mangy old Hereford bull!"

He looked odd. As if he'd tried to swallow a watermelon and couldn't get it down. He stood up, still staring at the crumpled check, and turned away. He walked to the sink, staring out the darkened window.

"How did you get a job decorating anything?"

"I studied for several years at an excellent school of interior design in New York," she said. "I got a job with one of the leading agencies and spent two years developing my craft. That's why I got so angry when you made the remark about interior decorators being con artists," she added. "You see, I am one."

"New York?"

"Yes. It's the best place to learn, and to work."

"And you got pneumonia . . ."

"And had to give it up temporarily," she agreed.

She frowned. He sounded strange. "Thanks to you, I'm back on my feet now and in fine form. The lady I did the design for was really pleased with my work, too. But the reason I did it was to get you enough money to pay off your note . . ."

"I can't take this," he said in a strained tone. He put it gently on the table and started out the door.

"But, Everett, your supper . . . !" she called.

"I'm not hungry." He kept walking. A moment later, the front door slammed behind him.

She sat there at the table, alone, staring at the check for a long time, until the numbers started to blur. Her eyes burned with unshed tears. She loved him. She loved Everett Culhane. And in the space of one night, her good intentions had lost her the pleasure of being near him. She knew almost certainly that he was going to fire her now. Too late, she remembered his opinion of city women. She hadn't had time to explain that it was her parents' idea for her to study and work in New York, not her own. Nor that the pressure had been too much. He thought it was only pneumonia. Could she convince him in time that she wasn't what he was sure she was? That she wanted to stay here forever, not just as a temporary thing? She glanced toward the door with a quiet sigh. Well, she'd just sit here and wait until the shock wore off and he came back.

She did wait. But when three o'clock in the morning came, with no sign of Everett, she went reluctantly upstairs and lay down. It didn't help that she still smelled leather and faint cologne, and that her mind replayed the fierce ardor she'd learned from him until, exhausted, she slept.

When her eyes slowly opened the next morning, she felt as if she hadn't slept at all. And the first thing she remembered was Everett's shocked face when she'd told him what she used to do for a living. She couldn't understand why he'd reacted that way. After the way it had been between them, she hadn't expected him to walk off without at least discussing it. She wondered if it was going to be that way until he fired her. Because she was sure he was going to. And she knew for a certainty that she didn't want to go. She loved him with all her heart.

Chapter Seven

If she'd hoped for a new start that morning, she was disappointed. She fixed breakfast, but Everett went out the front door without even sticking his head in the kitchen. Apparently, he'd rather have starved than eat what she'd cooked for him.

That morning set the pattern for the next two days. Jennifer cooked and wound up eating her efforts by herself. Everett came home in the early hours of the morning, arranging his schedule so that she never saw him at all.

He'd sold the bull. She found it out from Eddie, who was in a nasty temper of his own.

"I practically begged him to wait and see what happened," Eddie spat as he delivered the eggs to Jennifer the second morning. "When that neighbor didn't want the bull, Everett just loaded it up and took it to the sale without a word. He looks bad. He won't talk. Do you know what's eating him?"

She avoided that sharp look. "He's worried about money, I think," she said. "I offered him what I had. He got mad and stomped off and he hasn't spoken to me since."

"That don't sound like Everett."

"Yes, I know." She sighed, smiling at him. "I think he wants me to go away, Eddie. He's done everything but leave the ranch forever to get his point across."

"Money troubles are doing it, not you." Eddie grinned. "Don't back off now. He needs us all more than ever."

"Maybe he does," Jennifer said. "I just wish he'd taken the money I offered to lend him."

"That would be something, all right, to watch Everett take money from a lady. No offense, Miss Jenny, but he's too much man. If you know what I mean."

She did, unfortunately. She'd experienced the male in him, in ways that would haunt her forever. And worst of all was the fact that she was still hungry for him. If anything, that wild little interlude on the sofa had whetted her appetite, not satisfied it.

For lunch, she put a platter of cold cuts in the refrigerator and left a loaf of bread on the table along with a plate and cup; there was coffee warming on the stove. She pulled on a sweater and went down to visit Libby. It was like baiting a trap, she thought. Perhaps he'd enjoy eating if he didn't have to look at a city woman.

Libby didn't ask any obvious questions. She simply enjoyed the visit, since the children were in school and she could talk about clothes and television programs with the younger woman.

At one o'clock, Jennifer left the house and walked slowly back up to see if Everett had eaten. It was something of a shock to find him wandering wildly around the kitchen, smoking like a furnace.

"So there you are!" he burst out, glaring at her with menacing brown eyes. "Where in hell have you been? No note, no nothing! I didn't know if you'd left or been kidnapped, or stepped into a hole . . ."

"What would you care if I had?" she demanded. "You've made it obvious that you don't care for my company!"

"What did you expect?" he burst out, his eyes dangerous. "You lied to me."

"I didn't," she said in defense.

"I thought you were a poor little secretary in danger of starving if I didn't take you in," he said through his teeth. He let his eyes wander with slow insolence over the white blouse and green skirt she was wearing. "And what do I find out? That you lived and worked in New York at a job that would pay you more in one week than I can make here in two months!"

So that was it. His pride was crushed. He was poor and she wasn't, and that cut him up.

But knowing it wasn't much help. He was as unapproachable as a coiled rattler. In his dusty jeans and boots and denim shirt, he looked as wild as an outlaw.

"I had pneumonia," she began. "I had to come south . . ."

"Bobby didn't know?" he asked.

"No," she said. "I didn't see any reason to tell him. Everett . . . !"

"Why didn't you say something at the beginning?" he demanded, ramming his hand into his pocket to fish for another cigarette.

"What was there to say?" she asked impotently. She took the sweater from around her shoulders, and her green eyes pleaded with him. "Everett, I'm just the same as I always was."

"Not hardly," he said. His jaw clenched as he lit the cigarette. "You came here looking like a straggly little hen. And now . . . " He blew out a cloud of smoke, letting his eyes savor the difference. They lingered for a long time on her blouse, narrowing, burning. "I brought a city girl here once," he said absently. His eyes caught hers. "When she found out that I had more ideas than I had money, she turned around and ran. We were engaged," he said on a short laugh. "I do have the damndest blind spot about women."

She wrapped her arms around her chest. "Why does it make so much difference?" she asked. "I only took the designing job to help, Rett," she added. She moved closer. "I just wanted to pay you back, for giving me a job when I needed it. I knew you couldn't afford me, but I was in trouble, and you sacrificed for me." Her eyes searched his dark, hard face. "I wanted to do something for you. I wanted you to have your bull."

His face hardened and he turned away, as if he couldn't bear the sight of her. He raised the cigarette to his lips and his back was ramrod straight.

"I want you to leave," he said.

"Yes, I know," she said on a soft little sigh. "When?"

"At the end of the week."

So soon, she thought miserably? Her eyes clouded as she stared at his back, seeing the determination in every hard line of it. "Do you hate me?" she asked in a hurting tone.

He turned around slowly, the cigarette held tautly in one hand, and his eyes slashed at her. He moved closer, with a look in his dark eyes that was disturbing.

With a smooth motion, he tossed the unfinished cigarette into an ashtray on the table and reached for her.

"I could hate you," he said harshly. "If I didn't want you so damned much." He bent his head and caught her mouth with his.

She stiffened for an instant, because there was no tenderness in this exchange. He was rough and hurting, deliberately. Even so, she loved him. If

this was all he could give, then it would be enough.
She inched her trapped hands up to his neck and
slid them around it. Her soft mouth opened, giving
him all he wanted of it. She couldn't respond, he
left her no room. He was taking without any
thought of giving back the pleasure.

His hard hands slid roughly over her breasts and
down to her hips and ground her against him in a
deep, insolent rhythm, letting her feel what she
already knew—that he wanted her desperately.

"Was it all a lie?" he ground out against her
mouth. "Are you really a virgin?"

Her lips felt bruised when she tried to speak.
"Yes," she said shakily. He was still holding her
intimately, and when she tried to pull back, he only
crushed her hips closer.

"No, don't do that," he said with a cruel smile.
"I like to feel you. Doesn't it give you a sense of
triumph, city girl, knowing how you affect me?"

Her hands pushed futilely at his hard chest.
"Everett, don't make me feel cheap," she pleaded.

"Could I?" He laughed coldly. "With your pros-
pects?" His hands tightened, making her cry out.
His mouth lowered. This time it was teasing,
tantalizing. He brushed it against her own mouth in
whispery motions that worked like a narcotic,
hypnotizing her, weakening her. She began to
follow those hard lips with her own, trying to
capture them in an exchange that would satisfy the
ache he was creating.

"Do you want to stay with me, Jenny?" he whispered.

"Yes," she whispered back, her whole heart in her response. She clutched at his shirtfront with trembling fingers. Her mouth begged for his. "Yes, Everett, I want to stay . . . !"

His breath came hard and fast at her lips. "Then come upstairs with me, now, and I'll let you," he breathed.

It took a minute for his words to register, and then she realized that his hands had moved to the very base of her spine, to touch her in ways that shocked and frightened her.

She pulled against his hands, her face red, her eyes wild. "What do you mean?" she whispered.

He laughed, his eyes as cold as winter snow. "Don't you know? Sleep with me. Or would you like to hear it in a less formal way?" he added, and put it in words that made her hand come up like a whip.

He caught it, looking down at her with contempt and desire and anger all mixed up in his hard face. "Not interested?" he asked mockingly. "You were a minute ago. You were the other night, when you let me strip you."

Her teeth clenched as she tried to hang on to her dignity and her pride. "Let me go," she whispered shakily.

"I could please you, city girl," he said with a bold, slow gaze down her taut body. "You're going to give in to a man someday. Why not me? Or do I need to get rich first to appeal to you?"

Tears welled up in her eyes. His one hand was about to crack the delicate bone in her wrist, and the other was hurting her back. She closed her eyelids to shut off the sight of his cold face. She loved him so. How could he treat her this way? How could he be so cruel after that tenderness they'd shared!

"No comment?" he asked. He dropped his hands and retrieved his still-smoking cigarette from the ashtray. "Well, you can't blame a man for trying. You seemed willing enough the other night. I thought you might like some memories to carry away with you."

She'd had some beautiful ones, she thought miserably, until now. Her hands reached, trembling, for her sweater. She held it over her chest and wouldn't look up.

"I've got some correspondence on the desk you can type when you run out of things to do in the kitchen," he said, turning toward the door. He looked back with a grim smile on his lips. "That way you can make up some of the time you spent decorating that woman's house for her."

She still didn't speak, didn't move. The world had caved in on her. She loved him. And he could treat her like this, like some tramp he'd picked up on the street!

He drew in a sharp breath. "Don't talk, then,"

he said coldly. "I don't give a damn. I never did. I wanted you, that's all. But if I had the money, I could have you and a dozen like you, couldn't I?"

She managed to raise her ravaged face. He seemed almost to flinch at the sight of it, but he was only a blur through the tears in her eyes, and she might have been mistaken.

"Say something!" he ground out.

She lifted her chin. Her pale, swollen eyes just stared at him accusingly, and not one single word left her lips. Even if he threw her against the wall, she wouldn't give him the satisfaction of even one syllable!

He drew in a furious breath and whirled on his heel, slamming out the door.

She went upstairs like a zombie, hardly aware of her surroundings at all. She went into her room and took the uncashed checks that he'd signed for her salary and put them neatly on her dresser. She packed very quickly and searched in her purse. She had just enough pocket money left to pay a cab. She could cash the design firm's check in town when she got there. She called the cab company and then lifted her case and went downstairs to wait for it.

Everett was nowhere in sight, neither were Eddie and Bib, when the taxi came winding up the driveway. She walked down the steps, her eyes dry now, her face resolved, and got inside.

"Take me into town, please," she said quietly.

The cab pulled away from the steps, and she

scanned the ranchhouse and the corrals one last time. Then she turned away and closed her eyes. She didn't look back, not once.

Fortunately, Jennifer had no trouble landing a job. Sally Wade had been so impressed with the work that she'd done for Mrs. Whitehall that she practically created a position for Jennifer in her small, and still struggling, design firm. Jennifer loved the work, but several weeks had passed before she was able to think about Everett without crying.

The cup of coffee at Jennifer's elbow was getting cold. She frowned at it as her hand stilled on the sketch she was doing for a new client.

"Want some fresh?" Sally Wade asked from the doorway, holding her own cup aloft. "I'm just going to the pot."

"Bless you," Jennifer laughed.

"That's the first time you've really looked happy in the three months since you've been here," Sally remarked, cocking her head. "Getting over him?"

"Over whom?" came the shocked reply.

"That man, whoever he was, who had you in tears your first week here. I didn't pry, but I wondered," the older woman confessed. "I kept waiting for the phone to ring, or a letter to come. But nothing did. I kind of thought that he had to care, because you cared so much."

"He wanted a mistress," Jennifer said, putting it

into words. "And I wanted a husband. We just got our signals crossed. Besides," she added with a wan smile, "I'm feeling worlds better. I've got a great job, a lovely boss, and even a part-time boyfriend. If you can call Drew a boy."

"He's delightful." Sally sighed. "Just what you need. A live wire."

"And not a bad architect, either. You must be pleased he's working with us." She grinned. "He did a great job on that office project last month."

"So did you," Sally said, smiling. She leaned against the doorjamb. "I thought it a marvelous idea, locating a group of offices in a renovated mansion. It only needed the right team, and you and Drew work wonderfully well together."

"In business, yes." Jennifer twirled her pencil around in her slender fingers. "I just don't want him getting serious about me. If it's possible for him to get serious about anyone." She laughed.

"Don't try to bury yourself."

"Oh, I'm not. It's just . . ." She shrugged. "I'm only now getting over . . . I don't want any more risks. Not for a long time. Maybe not ever."

"Some men are kind-hearted," Sally ventured.

"So why are you single?" came the sharp reply.

"I'm picky," Sally informed her with a sly smile. "Very, very picky. I want Rhett Butler or nobody."

"Wrong century, wrong state."

"You're from Georgia. Help me out!"

"Sorry," Jennifer murmured. "If I could find one, do you think I'd tell anybody?"

"Point taken. Give me that cup and I'll fill it for you."

"Thanks, boss."

"Oh, boy, coffee!" a tall, redheaded man called from the doorway as he closed the door behind him. "I'll have mine black, with two doughnuts, a fried egg . . ."

"The breakfast bar is closed, Mr. Peterson," Jennifer told him.

"Sorry, Drew," Sally added. "You'll just have to catch your own chicken and do it the hard way."

"I could starve," he grumbled, ramming his hands in his pockets. He had blue eyes, and right now they were glaring at both women. "I don't have a wife or a mother. I live alone. My cook hates me . . ."

"You're breaking my heart," Sally offered.

"You can have the other half of my doughnut," Jennifer said, holding up a chunk of doughnut with chocolate clinging to it.

"Never mind." Drew sighed. "Thanks all the same, but I'll just wither away."

"That wouldn't be difficult," Jennifer told him. "You're nothing but skin and bones."

"I gained two pounds this week," he said, affronted.

"Where is it," Sally asked with a sweeping glance, "in your big toe?"

"Ha, ha," he laughed as she turned to go to the coffeepot.

"You *are* thin," Jennifer remarked.

He glared at her. "I'm still a growing boy." He stretched lazily. "Want to ride out to the new office building with me this morning?"

"No, thanks. I've got to finish these drawings. What do you think?"

She held one up, and he studied them with an architect's trained eye. "Nice. Just remember that this," he said, pointing to the vestibule, "is going to be a heavy-traffic area, and plan accordingly."

"There goes my white carpet," she teased.

"I'll white carpet you," he muttered. He pursed his lips as he studied her. "Wow, lady, what a change."

She blinked up at him. "What?"

"You. When you walked in here three months ago, you looked like a drowned kitten. And now . . ." He only sighed.

She was wearing a beige suit with a pink candy-striped blouse and a pink silk scarf. Her blond hair was almost platinum with its new body and sheen, and she'd had it trimmed so that it hung in wispy waves all around her shoulders. Her face was creamy and soft and she was wearing makeup again. She looked nice, and his eyes told her so.

"Thanks."

He pursed his lips. "What for?"

"The flattery," she told him. "My ego's been even with my ankles for quite awhile."

"Stick with me, kid, I'll get it all the way up to your ears," he promised with an evil leer.

"Sally, he's trying to seduce me!" she called toward the front of the office.

She expected some kind of bantering reply, but none was forthcoming. She looked up at Drew contemplatively. "Reckon she's left?"

"No. She's answered the phone. You still aren't used to the musical tone, are you?"

No, she wasn't. There were quite a lot of things she wasn't used to, and the worst of them was being without Everett. She had a good job, a nice apartment, and some new clothes. But without him, none of that mattered. She was going through the motions, and little more. His contempt still stung her pride when she recalled that last horrible scene. But she couldn't get him out of her mind, no matter how she tried.

"Well!" Sally said, catching her breath as she rejoined them. "If the rest of him looks like his voice, I may get back into the active part of the business. That was a potential client, and I think he may be the Rhett Butler I've always dreamed of. What a silky, sexy voice!"

"Dream on," Jennifer teased.

"He's coming by in the morning to talk to us. Wants his whole house done!" the older woman exclaimed.

"He must have a sizeable wallet, then," Drew remarked.

Sally nodded. "He didn't say where the house

was, but I assume it's nearby. It didn't sound like a long-distance call." She glanced at Jennifer with a smile. "Apparently your reputation has gotten around, too." she laughed. "He asked if you'd be doing the project. I had the idea he wouldn't have agreed otherwise." She danced around with her coffee cup in her hand. "What a godsend. With the office building and this job, we'll be out of the red, kids! What a break!"

"And you were groaning about the bills just yesterday,"Jennifer laughed. "I told you something would turn up, didn't I?"

"You're my lucky charm," Sally told her. "If I hadn't hired you, I shudder to think what would have happened."

"You know how much I appreciated getting this job," Jennifer murmured. "I was in pretty desperate circumstances."

"So I noticed. Well, we did each other a lot of good. We still are," Sally said warmly, "Hey, let's celebrate. Come on. I'll treat you two to lunch."

"Lovely!" Jennifer got up and grabbed her purse. "Come on, Drew, let's hurry before she changes her mind!"

She rushed out the door, with Drew in full pursuit, just ahead of Sally. And not one of them noticed the man sitting quietly in the luxury car across the street, his fingers idly caressing a car phone in the back seat as he stared intently after them.

Chapter Eight

Drew had asked Jennifer to go out with him that night, but she begged off with a smile. She didn't care for the nightlife anymore. She went to company functions with Sally when it was necessary to attract clients or discuss new projects, but that was about the extent of her social consciousness. She spent most of her time alone, in her modest apartment, going over drawings and planning rooms.

She enjoyed working for Sally. Houston was a big city, but much smaller than New York. And while there was competition, it wasn't as fierce. The pressure was less. And best of all, Jennifer was allowed a lot of latitude in her projects. She had a free hand to incorporate her own ideas as long as they complemented the client's requirements. She

loved what she did, and in loving it, she blossomed
into the woman she'd once been. But this time she
didn't allow herself to fall into the trap of over-
spending. She budgeted, right down to the pretty
clothes she loved—she bought them on sale, a few
at a time, and concentrated on mix-and-match
outfits.

It was a good life. But part of her was still
mourning Everett. Not a day went by when she
couldn't see him, tall and unnerving, somewhere in
her memory. They'd been so good for each other.
She'd never experienced such tenderness in a man.

She got up from the sofa and looked out at the
skyline of Houston. The city was bright and beautiful, but she remembered the ranch on starry nights.
Dogs would howl far in the distance, crickets would
sing at the steps. And all around would be open
land and stars and the silhouettes of Everett's
cattle.

She wrapped her arms around her body and
sighed. Perhaps someday the pain would stop and
she could really forget him. Perhaps someday she
could remember his harsh accusations and not be
wounded all over again. But right now, it hurt
terribly. He'd been willing to let her stay as his
mistress, as a possession to be used when he
wanted her. But he wouldn't let her be part of his
life. He couldn't have told her more graphically
how little he thought of her. That had hurt the
most. That even after all the caring, all the tender-

ness, she hadn't reached him at all. He hadn't seen past the shape of her body and his need of it. He hadn't loved her. And he'd made sure she knew it.

There were a lot of nights, like this one, when she paced and paced and wondered if he thought of her at all, if he regretted what had happened. Somehow, she doubted it. Everett had a wall like steel around him. He wouldn't let anyone inside it. Especially not a city woman with an income that could top his.

She laughed bitterly. It was unfortunate that she had fallen in love for the first time with such a cynical man. It had warped the way she looked at the world. She felt as if she, too, were impregnable now. Her emotions were carefully wrapped away, where they couldn't be touched. Nobody could reach her now. She felt safe in her warm cocoon. Of course, she was as incapable of caring now as he'd been. And in a way, that was a blessing. Because she couldn't be hurt anymore. She could laugh and carry on with Drew, and it didn't mean a thing. There was no risk in dating these days. Her heart was safely tucked away.

With a last uncaring look at the skyline, she turned off the lights and went to bed. Just as she drifted off, she wondered who the new client was going to be, and grinned at the memory of Sally's remark about his sexy voice.

She overslept the next morning for the first time in months. With a shriek as she saw the time, she dressed hastily in a silky beige dress and high heels. She moaned over her unruly hair that would curl and feather all around her shoulders instead of going into a neat bun. She touched up her face, stepped into her shoes, and rushed out into the chill autumn morning without a jacket or a sweater. Oh, well, maybe she wouldn't freeze, she told herself as she jumped into the cab she'd called and headed for the office.

"So there you are," Drew said with mock anger as she rushed breathlessly in the door, her cheeks flushed, her eyes sparkling, her hair disheveled and sexy around her face. "I ought to fire you."

"Go ahead. I dare you." She laughed up at him. "And I'll tell Sally all about that last expense voucher you faked."

"Blackmailer!" he growled. He reached out and lifted her up in the air, laughing at her.

"Put me down, you male chauvinist." She laughed gaily. Her face was a study in beauty, her body lusciously displayed in the pose, her hands on his shoulders, her hair swirling gracefully as she looked down at him. "Come on, put me down," she coaxed. "Put me down, Drew, and I'll take you to lunch."

"In that case," he murmured dryly.

"Jennifer! Drew!" Sally exclaimed, entering the room with a nervous laugh. "Stop clowning. We've got business to discuss, and you're making a horrible first impression."

"Oops," Drew murmured. He turned his head just as Jennifer turned hers, and all the laughter and brightness drained out of her like air out of a balloon. She stared down at the newcomer with strained features and eyes that went from shock to extreme anger.

Drew set her down on her feet and turned, hand extended, grinning. "Sorry about that. Just chastising the staff for tardiness." He chuckled. "I'm Andrew Peterson, resident architect. This is my associate, Jennifer King."

"I know her name," Everett Culhane said quietly. His dark eyes held no offer of peace, no hint of truce. They were angry and cold, and he smiled mockingly as his eyes went from Jennifer to Drew. "We've met."

Sally looked poleaxed. It had just dawned on her who Everett was, when she got a look at Jennifer's white face.

"Uh, Mr. Culhane is our new client," Sally said hesitantly. Jennifer looked as if she might faint. "You remember, Jenny, I mentioned yesterday that he'd called."

"You didn't mention his name," Jennifer said in a cool voice that shook with rage. "Excuse me, I have a phone call to make."

"Not so fast," Everett said quietly. "First we talk."

Her eyes glittered at him, her body trembled with suppressed tension. "I have nothing to say to you, Mr. Culhane," she managed. "And you have nothing to say to me that I care to hear."

"Jennifer . . . " Sally began nervously.

"If my job depends on working for Mr. Culhane, you can have my resignation on the spot," Jennifer said unsteadily. "I will not speak to him, much less work with him. I'm sorry."

She turned and went on wobbly legs to her office, closing the door behind her. She couldn't even sit down. She was shaking like a leaf all over and tears were burning her eyes. She heard voices outside, but ignored them. She stared at an abstract painting on the wall until she thought she'd go blind.

The sound of the door opening barely registered. Then it closed with a firm snap, and she glanced over her shoulder to find Everett inside.

It was only then that she noticed he was wearing a suit. A very expensive gray one that made his darkness even more formidable; his powerful body was streamlined and elegant in its new garments. He was holding a silverbelly Stetson in one lean hand and staring at her quietly, calculatingly.

"Please go away," she said with as much conviction as she could muster.

"Why?" he asked carelessly, tossing his hat onto her desk. He dropped into an armchair and crossed one long leg over the other. He lit a cigarette and pulled the ashtray on her desk closer, but his eyes never left her ravaged face.

"If you want your house redone, there are other

firms," she told him, turning bravely, although her legs were still trembling.

He saw that, and his eyes narrowed, his jaw tautened. "Are you afraid of me?" he asked quietly.

"I'm outraged," she replied in a voice that was little more than a whisper. Her hand brushed back a long, unruly strand of hair. "You might as well have taken a bullwhip to me, just before I left the ranch. What do you want now? To show me how prosperous you are? I've noticed the cut of your suit. And the fact that you can afford to hire this firm to redo the house does indicate a lot of money." She smiled unsteadily. "Congratulations. I hope your sudden wealth makes you happy."

He didn't speak for a long minute. His eyes wandered over her slowly, without any insult, as if he'd forgotten what she looked like and needed to stare at her, to fill his eyes. "Aren't you going to ask me how I came by it?" he demanded finally.

"No. Because I don't care," she said.

One corner of his mouth twitched a little. He took a draw from the cigarette and flicked an ash into the ashtray. "I sold off the oil rights."

So much for sticking to your principles, she wanted to say. But she didn't have the strength. She went behind her desk and sat down carefully.

"No comment?" he asked.

She blanched, remembering with staggering clarity the last time he'd said that. He seemed to remember it, too, because his jaw tautened and he drew in a harsh breath.

"I want my house done," he said curtly. "I want you to do it. Nobody else. And I want you to stay with me while you work on the place."

"Hell will freeze over first," she said quietly.

"I was under the impression that the firm wasn't operating in the black," he said with an insolent appraisal of her office. "The commission on this project will be pretty large."

"I told you once that you couldn't buy me," she said on a shuddering breath. "I'd jump off a cliff before I'd stay under the same roof with you!"

His eyes closed. When they opened again, he was staring down at his boot. "Is it that redheaded clown outside?" he asked suddenly, jerking his gaze up to catch hers.

Her lips trembled. "That's none of your business."

His eyes wandered slowly over her face. "You looked different with him," he said deeply. "Alive, vibrant, happy. And then, the minute you spotted me, every bit of life went out of you. It was like watching water drain from a glass."

"What did you expect, for God's sake!" she burst out, her eyes wild. "You cut me up!"

He drew in a slow breath. "Yes. I know."

"Then why are you here?" she asked wearily. "What do you want from me?"

He stared at the cigarette with eyes that barely saw it. "I told you. I want my house done." He looked up. "I can afford the best, and that's what I want. You."

There was an odd inflection in his voice, but she was too upset to hear it. She blinked her eyes, trying to get herself under control. "I won't do it. Sally will just have to fire me."

He got to his feet and loomed over the desk, crushing out the cigarette before he rammed his hands into his pockets and glared at her. "There are less pleasant ways to do this," he said. "I could make things very difficult for your new employer." His eyes challenged her. "Call my bluff. See if you can skip town with that on your conscience."

She couldn't, and he knew it. Her pride felt lacerated. "What do you think you'll accomplish by forcing me to come back?" she asked. "I'd put a knife in you if I could. I won't sleep with you, no matter what you do. So what will you get out of it?"

"My house decorated, of course," he said lazily. His eyes wandered over her. "I've got over the other. Out of sight, out of mind, don't they say?" He shrugged and turned away with a calculating look on his face. "And one body's pretty much like another in the dark," he added, reaching for his Stetson. His eyes caught the flutter of her lashes and he smiled to himself as he reached for the doorknob. "Well, Miss King, which is it? Do you come back to Big Spur with me or do I give Ms. Wade the sad news that you're leaving her in the lurch?"

Her eyes flashed green sparks at him. What choice was there? But he'd pay for this. Somehow, she'd make him. "I'll go," she bit off.

He didn't say another word. He left her office as though he were doing her a favor by letting her redecorate his house!

Sally came in the door minutes later, looking troubled and apologetic.

"I had no idea," she told Jennifer. "Honest to God, I had no idea who he was."

"Now you know," Jennifer said on a shaky laugh.

"You don't have to do it," the older woman said curtly.

"Yes, I'm afraid I do. Everett doesn't make idle threats," she said, rising. "You've been too good to me, Sally. I can't let him cause trouble for you on my account. I'll go with him. After all, it's just another job."

"You look like death warmed over. I'll send Drew with you. We'll do something to justify him . . ."

"Everett would eat him alive," she told Sally with a level stare. "And don't pretend you don't know it. Drew's a nice man but he isn't up to

Everett's weight or his temper. This is a private war."

"Unarmed combat?" Sally asked sadly.

"Exactly. He has this thing about city women, and I wasn't completely honest with him. He wants to get even."

"I thought revenge went out with the Borgias," Sally muttered.

"Not quite. Wish me luck. I'm going to need it."

"If it gets too rough, call for reinforcements," Sally said. "I'll pack a bag and move in with you, Everett or no Everett."

"You're a pal," Jennifer said warmly.

"I'm a rat," came the dry reply. "I wish I hadn't done this to you. If I'd known who he was, I'd never have told him you worked here."

Jennifer had hoped to go down to Big Spur alone, but Everett went back to her apartment with her, his eyes daring her to refuse his company.

He waited in the living room while she packed, and not one corner escaped his scrutiny.

"Looking for dust?" she asked politely, case in hand.

He turned, cigarette in hand, studying her. "This place must cost you an arm," he remarked.

"It does," she said with deliberate sarcasm. "But I can afford it. I make a lot of money, as you reminded me."

"I said a lot of cruel things, didn't I, Jenny

Wren?" he asked quietly, searching her shocked eyes. "Did I leave deep scars?"

She lifted her chin. "Can we go? The sooner we get there, the sooner I can get the job done and come home."

"Didn't you ever think of the ranch as home?" he asked, watching her. "You seemed to love it at first."

"Things were different then," she said noncommittally, and started for the door.

He took her case, his fingers brushing hers in the process, and producing electric results.

"Eddie and Bib gave me hell when they found out you'd gone," he said as he opened the door for her.

"I imagine you were too busy celebrating to notice."

He laughed shortly. "Celebrating? You damned little fool, I . . . !" He closed his mouth with a rough sigh. "Never mind. You might have left a nasty note or something."

"Why, so you'd know where I went?" she demanded. "That was the last thing I wanted."

"So I noticed," he agreed. He locked the door, handed her the key, and started down the hall toward the elevator. "Libby told me the name of the firm you'd worked for. It wasn't hard to guess you'd get a job with them."

She tossed her hair. "So that was how you found me."

"We've got some unfinished business," he replied as they waited for the elevator. His dark eyes held hers and she had to clench her fists to keep from kicking him. He had a power over her that all her anger couldn't stop. Deep beneath the layer of ice was a blazing inferno of hunger and love, but she'd die before she'd show it to him.

"I hate you," she breathed.

"Yes, I know you do," he said with an odd satisfaction.

"Mr. Culhane . . ."

"You used to call me Rett," he recalled, studying her. "Especially," he added quietly, "when we made love."

Her face began to color and she aimed a kick at his shins. He jumped back just as the elevator door opened.

"Pig!" she ground out.

"Now, honey, think of the kids," he drawled, aiming a glance at the elevator full of fascinated spectators. "If you knock me down, how can I support the ten of you?"

Red-faced, she got in ahead of him and wished with all her heart that the elevator doors would close right dead center on him. They didn't.

He sighed loudly, glancing down at her. "I begged you not to run off with that salesman," he said in a sad drawl. "I told you he'd lead you into a life of sin!"

There were murmured exclamations all around and a buzz of conversation. She glared up at him. Two could play that game.

"Well, what did you expect me to do, sit at home and knit while you ran around with that black-eyed hussy?" she drawled back. "And me in my delicate condition . . ."

"Delicate condition . . . ?" he murmured, shocked at her unexpected remark.

"And it's your baby, too, you animal," she said with a mock sob, glaring up at him.

"Darling!" he burst out. "You didn't tell me!"

And he grabbed her and kissed her hungrily right there in front of the whole crowd while she gasped and counted to ten and tried not to let him see that she was melting into the floor from the delicious contact with his mouth.

The elevator doors opened and he lifted his head as the other occupants filed out. He was breathing unsteadily and his eyes held hers. "No," he whispered when she tried to move away. His arm caught her and his head bent. "I need you," he whispered shakily. "Need you so . . . !"

That brought it all back. Need. He needed her. He just needed a body, that was all, and she knew it! She jerked herself out of his arms and stomped off the elevator.

"You try that again and I'll vanish!" she threatened, glaring up at him when they were outside the building. Her face was flushed, her breath shuddering. "I mean it! I'll disappear and you won't find me this time!"

He shrugged. "Suit yourself." He walked alongside her, all the brief humor gone out of his face. She wondered minutes later if it had been there at all.

Chapter Nine

He had a Lincoln now. Not only the car, but a driver to go with it. He handed her bag to the uniformed driver and put Jennifer in the back seat beside him.

"Aren't we coming up in the world, though?" she asked with cool sarcasm.

"Don't you like it?" he replied mockingly. He leaned back against the seat facing her and lit a cigarette. "I didn't think a woman alive could resist flashy money."

She remembered reluctantly how he'd already been thrown over once for the lack of wealth. Part of her tender heart felt sorry for him. But not any part that was going to show, she told herself.

"You could buy your share now, I imagine," she said, glancing out the window at the traffic.

He blew out a thin cloud of smoke. The driver climbed in under the wheel and, starting the powerful car, pulled out into the street.

"I imagine so."

She stared at the purse in her lap. "They really did find oil out there?" she asked.

"Sure did. Barrels and barrels." He glanced at her over his cigarette. "The whole damned skyline's cluttered with rigs these days. Metal grasshoppers." He sighed. "The cattle don't even seem to mind them. They just graze right on."

Wouldn't it be something if a geyser blew out under one of his prize Herefords one day, she mused. She almost told him, and then remembered the animosity between them. It had been a good kind of relationship that they'd had. If only Everett hadn't ruined it.

"It's a little late to go into it now," he said quietly. "But I didn't mean to hurt you that much. Once I cooled down, I would have apologized."

"The apology wouldn't have meant much after what you said to me!" she said through her teeth, flushing at the memory of the crude phrase.

He looked away. For a long minute he just sat and smoked. "You're almost twenty-four years old, Jenny," he said finally. "If you haven't heard words like that before, you're overdue."

"I didn't expect to hear them from you," she shot back, glaring at him. "Much less have you treat me with less respect than a woman you might have picked up on the streets with a twenty-dollar bill!"

"One way or another, I'd have touched you like that eventually!" he growled, glaring at her. "And don't sit there like lily white purity and pretend you don't know what I'm talking about. We were on the verge of becoming lovers that night on the sofa."

"You wouldn't have made me feel ashamed if it had happened that night," she said fiercely. "You wouldn't have made me feel cheap!"

He seemed about to explode. Then he caught himself and took a calming draw from the cigarette. His dark eyes studied the lean hand holding it. "You hurt me."

It was a shock to hear him admit it. "What?"

"You hurt me." His dark eyes lifted. "I thought we were being totally honest with each other. I trusted you. I let you closer than any other woman ever got. And then out of the blue, you hit me with everything at once. That you were a professional woman, a career woman. Worse," he added quietly, "a city woman, used to city men and city life and city ways. I couldn't take it. I'd been paying you scant wages, and you handed me that check . . ." He sighed wearily. "My God, I can't even tell you how I felt. My pride took one hell of a blow. I had nothing, and you were showing me graphically that you could outdo me on every front."

"I only wanted to help," she said curtly. "I wanted to buy you the damned bull. Sorry. If I had it to do all over again, I wouldn't offer you a dime."

"Yes, it shows." He sighed. He finished the cigarette and crushed it out. "Who's the redhead?"

"Drew? Sally told you. He's our architect. He has his own firm, of course, but he collaborates with us on big projects."

"Not on mine," he said menacingly, and his eyes darkened. "Not in my house."

She glared back. "That will depend on how much renovation the project calls for, I imagine."

"I won't have him on my place," he said softly.

"Why?"

"I don't like the way he looks at you," he said coldly. "Much less the way he makes free with his hands."

"I'm twenty-three years old," she reminded him. "And I like Drew, and the way he looks at me! He's a nice man."

"And I'm not," he agreed. "Nice is the last thing I am. If he ever touches you that way again when I'm in the same room, I'll break his fingers for him."

"Everett Donald Culhane!" she burst out.

His eyebrows arched. "Who told you my whole name?"

She looked away. "Never mind." she said, embarrassed.

His hand brushed against her hair, caressing it. "God, your hair is glorious," he said quietly. "It was nothing like this at the ranch."

She tried not to feel his touch. "I'd been ill," she managed.

"And now you aren't. Now you're . . . fuller and softer-looking. Even your breasts . . ."

"Stop it!" she cried, red-faced.

He let go of her hair reluctantly, but his eyes didn't leave her. "I'll have you, Jenny," he said quietly, his tone as soft as it had been that night when he was loving her.

"Only if you shoot me in the leg first!" she told him.

"Not a chance," he murmured, studying her. "I'll want you healthy and strong, so that you can keep up with me."

Her face did a slow burn again. She could have kicked him, but they were sitting down. "I don't want you!"

"You did. You will. I've got a whole campaign mapped out, Miss Jenny," he told her with amazing arrogance. "You're under siege. You just haven't realized it yet."

She looked him straight in the eye. "My grandfather held off a whole German company during World War I rather than surrender."

His eyebrows went up. "Is that supposed to impress me?"

"I won't be your mistress," she told him levelly. "No matter how many campaigns you map out or what kind of bribes or threats you try to use. I came with you to save Sally's business. But all this is to me is a job. I am not going to sleep with you."

His dark, quiet eyes searched over her face. "Why?"

Her lips opened and closed, opened again. "Because I can't do it without love," she said finally.

"Love isn't always possible," he said softly. "Sometimes, other things have to come first. Mutual respect, caring, companionship . . ."

"Can we talk about something else?" she asked tautly. Her fingers twisted the purse out of shape.

He chuckled softly. "Talking about sex won't get you pregnant."

"You've got money now. You can buy women," she ground out. "You said so."

"Honey, would you want a man you had to buy?" he asked quietly, studying her face.

Her lips parted. "Would I . . ." She searched his eyes. "Well, no."

"I wouldn't want a woman I had to buy," he said simply. "I'm too proud, Jenny. I said and did some harsh things to you," he remarked. "I can understand why you're angry and hurt about it. Someday I'll try to explain why I behaved that way. Right now, I'll settle for regaining even a shadow of the friendship we had. Nothing more. Despite all this wild talk, I'd never deliberately try to seduce you."

"Wouldn't you?" she asked bitterly. "Isn't that the whole point of getting me down here?"

"No." He lit another cigarette.

"You said you were going to . . ." she faltered.

"I want to," he admitted quietly. "God, I want to! But I can't quite take a virgin in my stride. Once, I thought I might," he confessed, his eyes searching her face. "That night . . . You were so eager, and I damned near lost my head when I realized that I could have you." He stared at the tip of his cigarette with blank eyes. "Would you have hated me if I hadn't been able to stop?"

Her eyes drilled into her purse. "There's just no point in going over it," she said in a studiously polite tone. "The past is gone."

"Like hell it's gone," he ground out. "I look at you and start aching." he said harshly.

Her lower lip trembled as she glared at him. "Then stop looking. Or take cold showers! Just don't expect me to do anything about it. I'm here to work, period!"

His eyebrows arched, and he was watching her with a faintly amused expression. "Where did you learn about cold showers?"

"From watching movies!"

"Is that how you learned about sex, from the movies?" he taunted.

"No, I learned in school! Sex education," she bit off.

"In my day, we had to learn it the hard way," he murmured. "It wasn't part of the core curriculum."

She glanced at him. "I can see you, doing extracurricular work in somebody's backseat."

He reached out and caught her hair again, tugging on it experimentally. "In a haystall, actually," he said, his voice low and soft and dark. Her head turned and he held her eyes. "She was two years older than I was, and she taught me the difference between sex and making love."

Her face flushed. He affected her in ways nobody else could. She was trembling from the bare touch of his fingers on her hair; her heart was beating wildly. How was she going to survive being in the same house with him?

"Everett . . ." she began.

"I'm sorry about what I said to you that last day, Jenny," he said quietly. "I'm sorry I made it into something cheap and sordid between us. Because that's the last thing it would have been if you'd given yourself to me."

She pulled away from him with a dry little laugh. "Oh, really?" she said shakenly, turning her eyes to the window. They were out of Houston now, heading south. "The minute you'd finished with me, you'd have kicked me out the door, and you know it, Everett Culhane. I'd have been no different from all the other women you've held in contempt for giving in to you."

"It isn't like that with you."

"And how many times have you told that story?" she asked sadly.

"Once. Just now."

He sounded irritated, probably because she wasn't falling for his practiced line. She closed her eyes and leaned her head against the cool window pane.

"I'd rather stay in a motel," she said, "if you don't mind."

"No way, lady," he said curtly. "The same lock's

still on your door, if you can't trust me that far. But staying at Big Spur was part of the deal you and I negotiated."

She turned her head to glance at his hard, set profile. He looked formidable again, all dark, flashing eyes and coldness. He was like the man she'd met that first day at the screen door.

"What would you have done, if I'd given in?" she asked suddenly, watching him closely. "What if I'd gotten pregnant?"

His head turned and his eyes glittered strangely. "I'd have gotten down on my knees and thanked God for it," he said harshly. "What did you think I'd do?"

Her lips parted. "I hadn't really thought about it."

"I want children. A yardful."

That was surprising. Her eyes dropped to his broad chest, to the muscles that his gray suit barely contained, and remembered how it was to be held against him in passion.

"Libby said you loved the ranch," he remarked.

"I did. When I was welcome."

"You still are."

"Do tell?" She cocked her head. "I'm a career woman, remember? And I'm a city girl."

His mouth tugged up. "I think city girls are sexy." His dark eyes traveled down to her slender legs encased in pink hose. "I didn't know you had legs, Jenny Wren. You always kept them in jeans."

"I didn't want you leering at me."

"Ha!" he shot back. "You knew that damned blouse was torn, the day you fell off your horse." His eyes dared her to dispute him. "You wanted my eyes on you. I'll never forget the way you looked when you saw me staring at you."

Her chest rose and fell quickly. "I was shocked."

"Shocked, hell. Delighted." He lifted the cigarette to his mouth. "I didn't realize you were a woman until then. I'd seen you as a kid. A little helpless thing I needed to protect." His eyes cut sideways and he smiled mockingly. "And then that blouse came open and I saw a body I'd have killed for. After that, the whole situation started getting impossible."

"So did you."

"I know," he admitted. "My brain was telling me to keep away, but my body wouldn't listen. You didn't help a hell of a lot, lying there on that couch with your mouth begging for mine."

"Well, I'm human!" she burst out furiously. "And I never asked you to start kissing me."

"You didn't fight me."

She turned away. "Can't we get off this subject?"

"Just when it's getting interesting?" he mused. "Why? Don't you like remembering it?"

"No, I don't!"

"Does he kiss you the way I did?" he asked shortly, jerking her around by the arm, his lean hand hurting. "That redhead, have you let him touch you like I did!"

"No!" she whispered, shocking herself with the disgust she put into that one, telling syllable.

His nostrils flared and his dark eyes traveled to the bodice of her dress, to her slender legs, her rounded hips, and all the way back up again to her eyes. "Why not?" he breathed unsteadily.

"Maybe I'm terrified of men now," she muttered.

"Maybe you're just terrified of other men," he whispered. "It was so good, when we touched each other. So good, so sweet . . . I rocked you under me and felt you respond, here . . ." His fingers brushed lightly against the bodice of her dress.

Coming to her senses all at once, she caught his fingers and pushed them away.

"No!" she burst out.

His fingers curled around her hand. He brought her fingers to his mouth and nibbled at them softly, staring into her eyes. "I can't even get in the mood with other women," he said quietly. "Three long months and I still can't sleep for thinking how you felt in my arms."

"Don't," she ground out, bending her head. "You won't make me feel guilty."

"That isn't what I want from you. Not guilt."

Her eyes came up. "You just want sex, don't you? You want me because I haven't been with anyone else!"

He caught her face in his warm hands and searched it while the forgotten cigarette between his fingers sent up curls of smoke beside her head.

"Someday, I'll tell you what I really want," he said, his voice quiet and soft and dark. "When you've forgotten, and forgiven what happened. Until then, I'll just go on as I have before." His mouth twisted. "Taking cold showers and working myself into exhaustion."

She wouldn't weaken; she wouldn't! But his hands were warm and rough, and his breath was smoky against her parted lips. And her mouth wanted his.

He bent closer, just close enough to torment her. His eyes closed. His nose touched hers.

She felt reckless and hungry; and all her willpower wasn't proof against him.

"Jenny," he groaned against her lips.

"Isn't . . . fair," she whispered shakily.

"I know." His hands were trembling. They touched her face as if it were some priceless treasure. His mouth trembled, too, while it brushed softly over hers. "Oh, God, I'll die if I don't kiss you . . . !" he whispered achingly.

"No . . ." But it was only a breath, and he took it from her with the cool, moist pressure of his hard lips.

She hadn't dreamed of kisses this tender, this soft. He nudged her mouth with his until it opened. She shuddered with quickly drawn breaths. Her eyes slid open and looked into his slitted ones.

"Oh," she moaned in a sharp whisper.

"Oh," he whispered back. His thumbs brushed her cheeks. "I want you. I want to lie with you and touch you and let you touch me. I want to make love with you and to you."

"Everett . . . you mustn't," she managed in a husky whisper as his mouth tortured hers. "Please, don't do this . . . to me. The driver . . ."

"I closed the curtain, didn't you notice?" he whispered.

She looked past him, her breath jerky and quick, her face flushed, her eyes wild.

"You see?" he asked quietly.

She swallowed, struggling for control. Her eyes closed and she pulled carefully away from his warm hands.

"No," she said then.

"All right." He moved back and finished his cigarette in silence.

She glanced at him warily, tucking back a loose strand of hair.

"There's nothing to be afraid of," he said, as if he sensed all her hidden fears. "I want nothing from you that you don't want to give freely."

She clasped her hands together. Her tongue touched her dry lips, and she could still taste him on them. It was so intimate that she caught her breath.

"I can't go with you," she burst out, all at once.

"Your door has a lock," he reminded her. "And I'll even give you my word that I won't force you."

Her troubled eyes sought his and he smiled reassuringly.

"Let me rephrase that," he said after a minute. "I won't take advantage of any . . . lapses. Is that better?"

She clutched her purse hard enough to wrinkle the soft leather wallet inside. "I hate being vulnerable!"

"Do you think I don't?" he growled, his eyes flashing. He crushed out his cigarette. "I'm thirty-five, and it's never happened to me before." He glared at her. "And it had to be with a damned virgin!"

"Don't you curse at me!"

"I wasn't cursing," he said harshly. He reached for another cigarette.

"Will you please stop that?" she pleaded. "I'm choking on the smoke as it is."

He made a rough sound and repocketed the cigarette. "You'll be carrying a noose around with you next."

"Not for your neck," she promised him with a sweet smile. "Confirmed bachelors aren't my cup of tea."

"Career women aren't mine."

She turned her eyes out the window. And for the rest of the drive to the ranch she didn't say another word.

The room he gave her was the one she'd had before. But she was surprised to see that the linen hadn't been changed. And the checks he'd written for her were just where she'd left them, on the dresser.

She stared at him as he set her bag down. "It's . . . you haven't torn them up," she faltered.

He straightened, taking off his hat to run a hand through his thick, dark hair. "So what?" he growled, challenge in his very posture. He towered over her.

"Well, I don't want them!" she burst out.

"Of course not," he replied. "You've got a good paying job now, don't you?"

Her chin lifted. "Yes, I do."

He tossed his hat onto the dresser and moved toward her.

"You promised!" she burst out.

"Sure I did," he replied. He reached out and jerked her up into his arms, staring into her eyes. "What if I lied?" he whispered gruffly. "What if I meant to throw you on that bed, and strip you, and make love to you until dawn?"

He was testing her. So that was how it was going to be. She stared back at him fearlessly. "Try it," she invited.

His mouth curled up. "No hysterics?"

"I stopped having hysterics the day that horse threw me and you got an anatomy lesson," she tossed back. "Go ahead, rape me."

His face darkened. "It wouldn't be rape. Not between you and me."

"If I didn't want you, it would be."

"Honey," he said softly, "you'd want me. Desperately."

She already did. The feel of him, the clean smell

of his body, the coiled strength in his powerful muscles were all working on her like drugs. But she was too afraid of the future to slide backwards now. He wanted her. But nothing more. And without love, she wanted nothing he had to offer.

"You promised," she said again.

He sighed. "So I did. Damned fool." He set her down on her feet and moved away with a long sigh to pick up his hat. His eyes studied her from the doorway. "Well, come on down when you're rested, and I'll have Consuelo fix something to eat."

"Consuelo?"

"My housekeeper." His eyes watched the expressions that washed over her face. "She's forty-eight, nicely plump, and happily married to one of my new hands. All right?"

"Did you hope I might be jealous?" she asked.

His broad chest rose and fell swiftly. "I've got a lot of high hopes about you. Care to hear a few of them?"

"Not particularly."

"That's what I was afraid of." He went out and closed the door behind him with an odd laugh.

Chapter Ten

Consuelo was a treasure. Small, dark, very quick around the kitchen, and Jennifer liked her on sight.

"It is good that you are here, senorita," the older woman said as she put food on the new and very elegant dining room table. "So nice to see the senor do something besides growl and pace."

Jennifer laughed as she put out the silverware. "Yes, now he's cursing at the top of his lungs," she mused, cocking her ear toward the window. "Hear him?"

It would have been impossible not to. He was giving somebody hell about an open gate, and Jennifer was glad it wasn't her.

"Such a strange man," Consuelo sighed, shaking her head. "The room he has given you, senorita, he would not let me touch it. Not to dust, not even to change the linen."

"Did he say why?" Jennifer asked with studied carelessness.

"No. But sometimes at night . . ." she hesitated.

"Yes?"

Consuelo shrugged at the penetrating look she got from the younger woman. "Sometimes at night, the senor, he would go up there and just sit. For a long time. I wonder, you see, but the only time I mention this strange habit, he says to mind my own business. So I do not question it."

How illuminating that was. Jennifer pondered on it long and hard. It was almost as if he'd missed her. But then, if he'd missed her, he'd have to care. And he didn't. He just wanted her because she was something different, a virgin. And perhaps because she was the only woman who'd been close to him for a long time. Under the same circumstances, it could very well have been any young, reasonably attractive woman.

He came in from the corral looking dusty and tired and out of humor. Consuelo glanced at him and he glared at her as he removed his wide-brimmed hat and sat down at the table with his chaps still on.

"Any comments?" he growled.

"Not from me, senor," Consuelo assured him. "As far as I am concerned, you can sit there in your overcoat. Lunch is on the table. Call if you need me."

Jennifer put a hand over her mouth to keep from laughing. Everett glared at her.

"My, you're in a nasty mood," she observed as she poured him a cup of coffee from the carafe. She filled her own cup, too.

"Pat yourself on the back," he returned.

She raised her eyebrows. "Me?"

"You." He picked up a roll and buttered it.

"I can leave?" she suggested.

"Go ahead."

She sat back in her chair, watching him. "What's wrong?" she asked quietly. "Something is."

"Bull died."

She caught her breath. "The big Hereford?"

He nodded. "The one I sold and then bought back when I leased the oil rights." He stared at his roll blankly. "The vet's going to do an autopsy. I want to know why. He was healthy."

"I'm sorry," she said gently. "You were very proud of him."

His jaw tautened. "Well, maybe some of those heifers I bred to him will throw a good bull."

She dished up some mashed potatoes and steak and gravy. "I thought heifers were cows that hadn't grown up," she murmured. "Isn't that what you told me?"

"Heifers are heifers until they're two years old and bred for the first time. Which these just were."

"Oh."

He glanced at her. "I'm surprised you'd remember that."

"I remember a lot about the ranch," she murmured as she ate. "Are you selling off stock before winter?"

"Not a lot of it," he said. "Now that I can afford to feed the herd."

"It's an art, isn't it?" she asked, lifting her eyes to his. "Cattle-raising, I mean, It's very methodical."

"Like decorating?" he muttered.

"That reminds me." She got up, fetched her sketch pad, and put it down beside his plate. "I did those before I came down. They're just the living room and kitchen, but I'd like to see what you think."

"You're the decorator," he said without opening it. "Do what you please."

She glared at him and put down her fork. "Everett, it's your house. I'd at least like you to approve the suggestions I'm making."

He sighed and opened the sketch pad. He frowned. His head came up suddenly. "I didn't know you could draw like this."

"It kind of goes with the job," she said, embarrassed.

"Well, you're good. Damned good. Is this what it will look like when you're finished?" he asked.

"Something like it. I'll do more detailed drawings if you like the basic plan."

"Yes, I like it," he said with a slow smile. He ran a finger over her depiction of the sofa and she remembered suddenly that instead of drawing in a new one, she'd sketched the old one. The one they'd lain on that night. . . .

She cleared her throat. "The kitchen sketch is just under that one."

He looked up. "Was that a Freudian slip, drawing that particular sofa?" he asked.

Her face went hot. "I'm human!" she grumbled.

His eyes searched hers. "No need to overheat, Miss King. I was just asking a question. I enjoyed what we did, too. I'm not throwing stones." He turned the page and pursed his lips. "I don't like the breakfast bar."

Probably because it would require the services of an architect, she thought evilly.

'Why?" she asked anyway, trying to sound interested.

He smiled mockingly. "Because, as I told you already, I won't have that redhead in my house."

She sighed angrily. "As you wish." She studied his hard face. "Will you have a few minutes to go over some ideas with me tonight? Or are you still trying to work yourself into an early grave?"

"Would you mind if I did, Jenny?" he mused.

"Yes. I wouldn't get paid," she said venomously.

He chuckled softly. "Hardhearted little thing. Yes, I'll have some free time tonight." He finished his coffee. "But not now." He got up from the table.

"I'm sorry about your bull."

He stopped by her chair and tilted her chin up.

"It will all work out," he said enigmatically. His thumb brushed over her soft mouth slowly, with electrifying results. She stared up with an expression that seemed to incite violence in him.

"Jenny," he breathed gruffly, and started to bend.

"Senor," Consuelo called, coming through the door in time to break the spell holding them, "do you want dessert now?"

"I'd have had it but for you, woman," he growled. And with that he stomped out the door, rattling the furniture as he went.

Consuelo stared after him, and Jennifer tried not to look guilty and frustrated all at once.

For the rest of the day, Jennifer went from room to room, making preliminary sketches. It was like a dream come true. For a long time, ever since she'd first seen the big house, she'd wondered what it would be like to redo it. Now she was getting the chance, and she was overjoyed. The only sad part was that Everett wouldn't let her get Drew in to do an appraisal of the place. It would be a shame to redo it if there were basic structural problems.

That evening after a quiet supper she went into the study with him and watched him build a fire in the fireplace. It was late autumn and getting cold at night. The fire crackled and burned in orange and yellow glory and smelled of oak and pine and the whole outdoors.

"How lovely," she sighed, leaning back in the

armchair facing it with her eyes closed. She was wearing jeans again, with a button-down brown patterned shirt, and she felt at home.

"Yes," he said.

She opened her eyes lazily to find him standing in front of her, staring quietly at her face.

"Sorry, I drifted off," she said quickly, and started to rise.

"Don't get up. Here." He handed her the sketch pad and perched himself on the arm of the chair, just close enough to drive her crazy with the scent and warmth and threat of his big body. "Show me."

She went through the sketches with him, showing the changes she wanted to make. When they came to his big bedroom, her voice faltered as she suggested new Mediterranean furnishings and a king-sized bed.

"You're very big," she said, trying not to look at him. "And the room is large enough to accommodate it."

"By all means," he murmured, watching her. "I like a lot of room."

It was the way he said it. She cleared her throat. "And I thought a narrow chocolate-and-vanilla-stripe wallpaper would be nice. With a thick cream carpet and chocolate-colored drapes."

"Am I going to live in the room, or eat it?"

"Hush. And you could have a small sitting area if you like. A desk and a chair, a lounge chair . . ."

"All I want in my bedroom is a bed," he grumbled. "I can work down here."

"All right." She flipped the page, glad to be on to the next room, which was a guest bedroom. "This . . ."

"No."

She glanced up. "What?"

"No. I don't want another guest room there." He looked down into her eyes. "Make it into a nursery."

She felt her body go cold. "A nursery?"

"Well, I've got to have someplace to put the kids," he said reasonably.

"Where are they going to come from?" she asked blankly.

He sighed with exaggerated patience. "First you have a man. Then you have a woman. They sleep together and—"

"I know that!"

"Then why did you ask me?"

"Forgive me if I sound dull, but didn't you swear that you'd rather be dead than married?" she grumbled.

"Sure. But being rich has changed my ideas around. I've decided that I'll need somebody to leave all this to." He pulled out a cigarette and lit it.

She stared at her designs with unseeing eyes. "Do you have a candidate already?" she asked with a forced laugh.

"No, not yet. But there are plenty of women around." His eyes narrowed as he studied her profile. "As a matter of fact, I had a phone call last week. From the woman I used to be engaged to. Seems her marriage didn't work out. She's divorced now."

That hurt. She hadn't expected that it would, but it went through her like a dagger. "Oh?" she said. Her pencil moved restlessly on the page as she darkened a line. "Were you surprised?"

"Not really," he said with cynicism. "Women like that are pretty predictable. I told you how I felt about buying them."

"Yes." She drew in a slow breath. "Well, Houston is full of debutantes. You shouldn't have much trouble picking out one."

"I don't want a child."

She glanced up. "Picky, aren't you?"

His mouth curled. "Yep."

She laughed despite herself, despite the cold that was numbing her heart. "Well, I wish you luck. Now, about the nursery, do you want it done in blue?"

"No. I like girls, too. Make it pink and blue. Or maybe yellow. Something unisex." He got up, stretching lazily, and yawned. "God, I'm tired. Honey, do you mind if we cut this short? I'd dearly love a few extra hours' sleep."

"Of course not. Do you mind if I go ahead with the rooms we've discussed?" she asked. "I could go ahead and order the materials tomorrow. I've already arranged to have the wallpaper in the living room stripped."

"Go right ahead." He glanced at her. "How long do you think it will take, doing the whole house?"

"A few weeks, that's all."

He nodded. "Sleep well, Jenny. Good night."

"Good night."

He went upstairs, and she sat by the fire until it went out, trying to reconcile herself to the fact that Everett was going to get married and have children. It would be to somebody like Libby, she thought. Some nice, sweet country girl who had no ambition to be anything but a wife and mother. Tears dripped down her cheeks and burned her cool flesh. What a pity it wouldn't be Jennifer.

She decided that perhaps Everett had had the right idea in the first place. Exhaustion was the best way in the world to keep one's mind off one's troubles. So she got up at dawn to oversee the workmen who were tearing down wallpaper and repairing plaster. Fortunately the plasterwork was in good condition and wouldn't have to be redone. By the time they were finished with the walls, the carpet people had a free day and invaded the house. She escaped to the corral and watched Eddie saddlebreak one of the new horses Everett had bought.

Perched on the corral fence in her jeans and blue sweatshirt, with her hair in a ponytail, she looked as outdoorsy as he did.

"How about if I yell 'ride 'em, cowboy,' and cheer you on, Eddie?" she drawled.

He lifted a hand. "Go ahead, Miss Jenny!"

"Ride 'em, cowboy!" she hollered.

He chuckled, bouncing around on the horse. She was so busy watching him that she didn't even hear Everett ride up behind her. He reached out a long arm and suddenly jerked her off the fence and into the saddle in front of him.

"Sorry to steal your audience, Eddie," he yelled toward the older man, "but she's needed!"

Eddie waved. Everett's hard arm tightened around her waist, tugging her stiff body back into the curve of his, as he urged the horse into a canter.

"Where am I needed?" she asked, peeking over her shoulder at his hard face.

"I've got a new calf. Thought you might like to pet it."

She laughed. "I'm too busy to pet calves."

"Sure. Sitting around on fences like a rodeo girl." His arm tightened. "Eddie doesn't need an audience to break horses."

"Well, it was interesting."

"So are calves."

She sighed and let her body slump back against his. She felt him stiffen at the contact, felt his breath quicken. She could smell him, and feel him, and her body sang at the contact. It had been such a long time since those things had disturbed her.

"Where are we going?" she murmured contentedly.

"Down to the creek. Tired?"

"Ummm," she murmured. "My arms ache."

"I've got an ache of my own, but it isn't in my arms," he mused.

She cleared her throat and sat up straight. "Uh, what kind of calf is it?"

He laughed softly. "I've got an ache in my back from lifting equipment," he said, watching her face burn. "What did you think I meant?"

"Everett," she groaned, embarassed.

"You babe in the woods," he murmured. His fingers spread on her waist, so long that they trespassed onto her flat stomach as well. "Hold on."

He put the horse into a gallop and she caught her breath, turning in the saddle to cling to his neck and hide her face in his shoulder.

He laughed softly, coiling his arm around her. "I won't let you fall," he chided.

"Do we have to go so fast?"

"I thought you were in a hurry to get there." He slowed the horse as they reached a stand of trees beside the creek. Beyond it was a barbed-wire fence. Inside it was a cow and a calf, both Herefords.

He dismounted and lifted Jenny down. "She's gentle," he said, taking her hand to pull her along toward the horned cow. "I raised this one myself, from a calf. Her mama died of snakebite and I nursed her with a bottle. She's been a good breeder. This is her sixth calf."

The furry little thing fascinated Jenny. It had pink eyes and a pink nose and pink ears, and the rest of it was reddish-brown and white.

She laughed softly and rubbed it between the eyes. "How pretty," she murmured. "She has pink eyes!"

"He," he corrected. "It will be a steer."

She frowned. "Not a bull?"

He glowered down at her. "Don't you ever listen to me? A steer is a bull that's been converted for beef. A bull has . . ." He searched for the words. "A bull is still able to father calves."

She grinned up at him. "Not embarrassed, are you?" she taunted.

He cocked an eyebrow. "You're the one who gets embarrassed every time I talk straight," he said curtly.

She remembered then, and her smile faded. She touched the calf gently, concentrating on it instead of him.

His lean hands caught her waist and she gasped, stiffening. His breath came hard and fast at her back.

"There's a party in Victoria tomorrow night. One of the oil men's giving it. He asked me to come." His fingers bit into her soft flesh. "How about going with me and holding my hand? I don't know much about social events."

"You don't really want to go, do you?" she asked, looking over her shoulder at him knowingly.

He shook his head. "But it's expected. One of the penalties of being well-off. Socializing."

"Yes, I'll be very proud to go with you."

"Need a dress? I'll buy you one, since it was my idea."

She lowered her eyes. "No, thank you. I . . . I have one at my apartment, if you'll have someone drive me up there."

"Give Ted the key. He'll pick it up for you," he said, naming his chauffeur, who was also the new yardman.

"All right."

"Is it white?" he asked suddenly.

She glared at him. "No. It's black. Listen here, Everett Culhane, just because I've never . . . !"

He put a finger over her lips, silencing her. "I like you in white," he said simply. "It keeps me in line," he added with a wicked, slow smile.

"You just remember the nice new wife you'll have and the kids running around the house, and that will work very well," she said with a nip in her voice. "Shouldn't we go back? The carpet-layers may have some questions for me."

"Don't you like kids, Jenny?" he asked softly.

"Well, yes."

"Could you manage to have them and a career at the same time?" he asked with apparent indifference.

Her lips pouted softly. "Lots of women do," she said. "It's not the dark ages."

He searched her eyes. "I know that. But there are men who wouldn't want a working wife."

"Cavemen," she agreed.

He chuckled. "A woman like you might make a man nervous in that respect. You're pretty. Suppose some other man snapped you up while you were decorating his house? That would be hell on your husband's nerves."

"I don't want to get married," she informed him.

His eyebrows lifted. "You'd have children out of wedlock?"

"I didn't say that!"

"Yes, you did."

"Everett!" Her hands pushed at his chest. He caught them and lifted them slowly around his neck, tugging so that her body rested against his.

"Ummmm," he murmured on a smile, looking down at the softness of her body. "That feels nice. What were you saying, about children?"

"If . . . if I wanted them, then I guess I'd get married. But I'd still work. I mean . . . Everett, don't . . ." she muttered when he slid his hands down to her waist and urged her closer.

"Okay. You'd still work?"

His hands weren't pushing, but they were doing something crazy to her nerves. They caressed her back lazily, moving up to her hair to untie the ribbon that held it back.

"I'd work when the children started school. That was what I meant . . . will you stop that?" she grumbled, reaching back to halt his fingers.

He caught her hands, arching her so that he could look down and see the vivid tautness of her breasts against the thin fabric of her blouse.

"No bra?" he murmured, and the smile got bigger. "My, my, another Freudian slip?"

"Will you stop talking about bras and slips and let go of my hands, Mr. Culhane?" she asked curtly.

"I don't think you really want me to do that, Jenny," he murmured dryly.

"Why?"

"Because if I let go of your hands, I have to put mine somewhere else." He looked down pointedly at her blouse. "And there's really only one place I want to put them right now."

Her chest rose and fell quickly, unsteadily. His closeness and the long abstinence and the sun and warmth of the day were all working on her. Her eyes met his suddenly and the contact was like an electric jolt. All the memories came rushing back, all the old hungers.

"Do you remember that day you fell off the horse?" he asked in a soft, low tone, while bees buzzed somewhere nearby. "And your blouse came open, and I looked down and you arched your back so that I could see you even better."

Her lips parted and she shook her head nervously.

"Oh, but you did," he breathed. "I'd seen you, watching my mouth, wondering . . . and that day, it all came to a head. I looked at you and I wanted you. So simply. So hungrily. I barely came to my senses in time, and before I did, I was hugging the life out of you. And you were letting me."

She remembered that, too. It had been so glorious, being held that way.

He let go of her hands all at once and slid his arms around her, half lifting her off her feet. "Hard, Jenny," he whispered, drawing her slowly to him, so that she could feel her breasts flattening against his warm chest. It was like being naked against him.

She caught her breath and moaned. His cheek slid against hers and he buried his face in her throat. His arms tightened convulsively. And he rocked her, and rocked her, and she clung to him while all around them the wind blew and the sun burned, and the world seemed to disappear.

His breath came roughly and his arms trembled. "I don't feel this with other women," he said after a while. "You make me hungry."

"As you keep reminding me," she whispered back, "I'm not on the menu."

"Yes, I know." He brushed his mouth against her throat and then lifted his head and slowly released her. "No more of that," he said on a rueful sigh, "unless you'd like to try making love on horseback. I've got a man coming to see me about a new bull."

Her eyes widened. "Can people really make . . ." She turned away, shaking her head.

"I don't know," he murmured, chuckling at her shyness. "I've never tried it. But there's always a first time."

"You just keep your hands to yourself," she cautioned as he put her into the saddle and climbed up behind her.

"I'm doing my best, honey," he said dryly. He reached around her to catch the reins and his arm moved lazily across her breasts, feeling the hardened tips. "Oh, Jenny," he breathed shakily, "next time you'd better wear an overcoat."

She wanted to stop him, she really did. But the feel of that muscular forearm was doing terribly exciting things to her. She felt her muscles tauten in a dead giveaway.

She knew it was going to happen even as he let go of the reins and his hands slid around her to lift and cup her breasts. She let him, turning her cheek against his chest with a tiny cry.

"The sweetest torture on earth," he whispered unsteadily. His hands were so tender, so gentle. He made no move to open the blouse, although he must have known that he could, that she would have let him. His lips moved warmly at her temple. "Jenny, you shouldn't let me touch you like this."

"Yes, I know," she whispered huskily. Her hands moved over his to pull them away, but they lingered on his warm brown fingers. Her head moved against his chest weakly.

"Do you want to lie down on the grass with me

and make love?" he asked softly. "We could, just for a few minutes. We could kiss and touch each other, and nothing more."

She wanted to. She wanted it more than she wanted to breathe. But it was too soon. She wasn't sure of him. She only knew that he wanted her desperately and that she didn't dare pave the way for him. It was just a game to him. It kept him from getting bored while he found himself a wife. She loved him, but love on one side would never be enough.

"No, Rett," she said, although the words were torn from her. She moved his hands gently down, to her waist, and pressed them there. "No."

He drew away in a long, steady breath. "Level-headed Jenny," he said finally. "Did you know?"

"Know what?"

"That if I'd gotten you on the grass, nothing would have saved you?"

She smiled ruefully. "It was kind of the other way around." She felt him shudder, and she turned and pressed herself into his arms. "I want you, too. Please don't do this to me. I can't be what you want. Please, let me decorate your house and go away. Don't hurt me any more, Rett."

He lifted and turned her so that she was lying across the saddle in his arms. He held her close and took the reins in his hand. "I'm going to have to rethink my strategy, I'm afraid." He sighed. "It isn't working."

She looked up. "What do you mean?"

He searched her eyes and bent and kissed her forehead softly. "Never mind, kitten. You're safe now. Just relax. I'll take you home."

She snuggled close and closed her eyes. This was a memory she'd keep as long as she lived, of riding across the meadow in Everett's arms on a lovely autumn morning. His wife would have other memories. But this one would always be her own, in the long, lonely years ahead. Her hand touched his chest lightly, and her heart ached for him. If only he could love her back. But love wasn't a word he trusted anymore, and she couldn't really blame him. He'd been hurt too much. Even by her, when she hadn't meant to. She sighed bitterly. It was all too late. If only it had been different. Tears welled up in her eyes. If only.

Chapter Eleven

Jennifer wished for the tenth time that she'd refused Everett's invitation to the exclusive party in Victoria. It seemed that every single, beautiful woman in the world had decided to converge on the spot just to cast her eyes at Everett.

He did look good, Jennifer had to admit. There just wasn't anybody around who came close to matching him. Dressed in an elegant dinner jacket, he looked dark and debonair and very sophisticated. Not to mention sexy. The way the jacket and slacks fit, every muscle in that big body was emphasized in the most masculine way. It was anguish just to look at him; it was even worse to remember how it was to be held and touched by him. Jennifer felt her body tingle from head to toe at the memory of the day before, of his hands smoothing over her body, his voice husky and deep in her ear. And now there he stood making eyes at a gorgeous brunette.

She turned away and tossed down the entire contents of her brandy glass. If she hadn't been so tired from overworking herself, the brandy might not have been as potent. But it was her second glass and, despite the filling buffet, she was feeling the alcohol to a frightening degree. She kept telling herself that she didn't look bad herself, with her blond hair hanging long and loose around the shoulders of her low-cut clinging black dress. She was popular enough. So why didn't Everett dance one dance with her?

By the time she was danced around the room a couple of times by left-footed oilmen and dashing middle-aged married men, she felt like leaping over the balcony. How odd that at any party there were never any handsome, available bachelors.

"Sorry to cut in, but I have to take Jenny home," Everett said suddenly, cutting out a balding man in his fifties who was going over and over the latest political crisis with maddening intricacy.

Jennifer almost threw herself on Everett in gratitude. She mumbled something polite and completely untrue to the stranger, smiled, and stumbled into Everett's arms.

"Careful, honey, or we'll both wind up on the floor." He laughed softly. "Are you all right?"

"I'm just fine." She sighed, snuggling close. Her arms slid around him. "Everett, can I go to sleep now?"

He frowned and pulled her head up. "How much have you had to drink?"

"I lost count." She grinned. Her eyes searched his face blearily. "Gosh, Rett, you're so sexy."

A red stain highlighted his cheekbones. "You're drunk, all right. Come on."

"Where are we going?" she protested. "I want to dance."

"We'll dance in the car."

She frowned. "We can't stand up in there," she said reasonably.

He held her hand, tugging her along. They said good night to a couple she vaguely recognized as their hosts; then he got their coats from the maid and hustled her out into the night.

"Cold out here," she muttered. She nudged herself under his arm and pressed against his side with a sigh. "Better."

"For whom?" he ground out. His chest rose and fell heavily. "I wish I'd let Ted drive us."

"Why?" she murmured, giggling. "Are you afraid to be alone with me? You can trust me, honey," she said, nudging him. "I wouldn't seduce you, honest."

A couple passed them going down the steps, and the elderly woman gave Jennifer a curious look.

"He's afraid of me," Jennifer whispered. "He isn't on the pill, you see . . ."

"Jenny!" he growled, jerking her close.

"Not here, Rett!" she exclaimed. "My goodness, talk about impatience . . . !"

He was muttering something about a gag as he half-led, half-dragged her to the car.

"You old stick-in-the-mud, you." She laughed after he'd put her inside and climbed in next to her. "Did I embarrass you?"

He only glanced at her as he started the Lincoln. "You're going to hate yourself in the morning when I remind you what you've been saying. And I will," he promised darkly. "Ten times a day."

"You look gorgeous when you're mad," she observed. She moved across the seat and nuzzled close again. "I'll sleep with you tonight, if you like," she said gaily.

He stiffened and muttered something under his breath.

"Well, you've been trying to get me into bed with you, haven't you?" she asked. "Propositioning me that last day at the ranch, and then coming after me, and making all sorts of improper remarks . . . so now I agree, and what do you do? You get all red in the face and start cussing. Just like a man. The minute you catch a girl, you're already in pursuit of someone else, like that brunette you were dancing with," she added, glaring up at him. "Well, just don't expect that what you see is what you get, because I was in the ladies' room with her, and it's padded! I saw!"

He was wavering between anger and laughter. Laughter won. He started, and couldn't seem to stop.

"You won't think it's very funny if you take her out," she kept on, digging her own grave. Everything was fuzzy and pink and very pleasant. She felt so relaxed! "She's even smaller than I am," she muttered. "And her legs are just awful. She pulled up her skirt to fix her stockings . . . she hardly has any legs, they're so skinny!"

"Meow," he taunted.

She tossed back her long hair, and leaned her head back against the seat. Her coat had come open, revealing the deep neckline of the black dress. "Why won't you make love to me?"

"Because if I did, you'd scream your head off," he said reasonably. "Here, put your tired little head on my shoulder and close your eyes. You're soaked, honey."

She blinked. "I am not. It isn't raining."

He reached out an arm and pulled her against him. "Close your eyes, sweet," he said in a soft, tender tone. "I'll take good care of you."

"Will you sleep with me?" she murmured, resting her head on his shoulder

"If you want me to."

She smiled and closed her eyes with a long sigh. "That would be lovely," she whispered. And it was the last thing she said.

* * *

Morning came with blinding light and some confounded bird twittering his feathered head off outside the window.

"Oh, go away!" she whispered, and held her head. "An axe," she groaned. "There's an axe between my eyes. Bird, shut up!"

Soft laughter rustled her hair. She opened her eyes. Laughter?

Her head turned on the pillow and Everett's eyes looked back into her own. She gasped and tried to sit up, then groaned with the pain and fell back down again.

"Head hurt? Poor baby."

"You slept with me?" she burst out. She turned her head slowly to look at him. He was fully dressed, except for his shoes and jacket. He even had his shirt on. He was lying on top of the coverlet, and she was under it.

Slowly, carefully, she lifted the cover and looked. Her face flamed scarlet. She was dressed in nothing but a tiny pair of briefs. The rest of her was pink and tingling.

"Rett!" she burst out, horrified.

"I only undressed you," he said, leaning on an elbow to watch her. "Be reasonable, honey. You couldn't sleep in your evening gown. And," he added with a faint grin, "it wasn't my fault that you didn't have anything on under it. You can't imagine how shocked I was."

"That's right, I can't," she agreed, and her eyes accused him.

"I confess I did stare a little," he murmured. His hand brushed the unruly blond hair out of her eyes. "A lot," he corrected. "My God, Jenny," he said on a slow breath, "you are the most glorious sight undressed that I ever saw in my life. I nearly fainted."

"Shame on you!" she said, trying to feel outraged. It was difficult, because she was still tingling from the compliment.

"For what? For appreciating something beautiful?" He touched her nose with a long, lean finger. "Shame on you, for being embarrassed. I was a perfect gentleman. I didn't even touch you, except to put you under the covers."

"Oh."

"I thought I'd wait until you woke up, and do it then," he added with a grin.

Her fingers grabbed the covers tightly. "Oh, no, you don't!"

He moved closer, his fingers tangling in her blond hair as he loomed above her. "You had a lot to say about that brunette. Or don't you remember?"

She blinked. Brunette? Vaguely she remembered saying something insulting about the woman's body. Then she remembered vividly. Her face flamed.

"Something about how little she was, if I recall," he murmured dryly.

She bit her lower lip and her eyes met his uneasily. "Did I? How strange. Was she short?"

"That wasn't what you meant," he said. One lean hand moved down her shoulder and over the covers below her collarbone. "You meant, here, she was small."

If she looked up, she'd be finished. But she couldn't help it. Her eyes met his and the world seemed to narrow down to the two of them. She loved him so. Would it be wrong to kiss him just once more, to feel that hard, wonderful mouth on her own?

He seemed to read that thought, because his jaw tautened and his breathing became suddenly ragged. "The hell with being patient," he growled, reaching for the covers. "Come here."

He stripped them away and jerked her into his arms, rolling over with her, so that she was lying on him. Where his shirt was undone, her body pressed nakedly into his hairy chest.

His eyes were blazing as they looked up into hers. He deliberately reached down to yank his shirt away, his eyes on the point where her soft breasts were crushed against his body. Dark and light, she thought shakily, looking at the contrast between his dark skin and her pale flesh.

But still he didn't touch her. His hands moved up into her hair, oddly tender, at variance with the tension she could feel in his body.

"Don't you want . . . to touch me?" she whispered nervously.

"More than my own life," he confessed. "But I'm not going to. Come down here and kiss me."

"Why not?" she whispered, bending to give him her mouth.

"Because Consuelo's on her way up the stairs with coffee and toast," he breathed. "And she never knocks."

She sat up with a gasp. "Why didn't you say so!"

He laughed softly, triumphantly, his eyes eating her soft body as she climbed out of the bed and searched wildly for a robe.

"Here," he murmured, throwing his long legs over the bed. He reached under her pillow and got her nightgown. "Come here and I'll stuff you in it."

She didn't even question the impulse that made her obey him instantly. She lifted her arms as he held the nightgown over her head and gasped as he bent first and kissed her rosy breasts briefly, but with a tangible hunger. While she was getting over the shock, he tugged the long cotton gown over her head, lifted her, tossed her into the bed, and pulled the covers over her with a knowing smile.

And Consuelo opened the door before she could get out a word.

"Good morning!" The older woman laughed, handing the tray to Everett. "Also is hair of the dog, in the glass," she added with a wry glance at Jennifer. "To make the senorita's head a little better."

And she was gone as quickly as she'd come. Everett put the tray down beside Jennifer on the bed and poured cream into her coffee.

"Why did you do that?" she whispered, still shaking from the wild little caress.

"I couldn't help myself," he murmured, smiling at her. "I've wanted to, for a long time."

She took the coffee in trembling hands. He steadied them, watching her shaken features.

"It's part of lovemaking," he said softly. "Nothing sordid or shameful. When we make love, that's how I'll rouse you before I take you."

She shuddered, and the coffee cup began to rock again. Her eyes, meeting his, were wild with mingled fear and hunger.

"Except," he added quietly, "that I won't stop at the waist."

Coffee went everywhere. She cursed and muttered and grumbled and moped. But when she raised her glittering eyes to his the pupils dilated until they were almost black.

He laughed softly, menacingly. "Almost," he said enigmatically. "Almost there." He got up, "I'll get Consuelo to come and help you mop up." He turned with one hand on the doorknob, impossibly attractive, wildly sensuous with his hair ruffled and his shirt open and his bare, muscular chest showing. "The brunette was Jeb Doyle's daughter," he added. "She's looking for a husband. She rides like a man, she loves cattle and kids, she's twenty-eight and she lives about five miles south of here. She may be small, but she's got nice, full hips. Just right for having children. Her name's Sandy."

She was getting madder by the second. He was baiting her! She picked up the coffee cup and, without even thinking, threw it at him.

It shattered against the closed door. He went down the hall laughing like a banshee and she screamed after him. By the time Consuelo got to her, the rest of the coffee and the headache remedy had turned the bedspread a strange shade of tan.

For the next week, she gave Everett the coldest shoulder she could manage. He was gone from the ranch frequently, and she noticed it and remembered what he'd said about the brunette, and wanted desperately to kill him. No, not just kill him. Torture him. Slowly. Over an open fire.

It got worse. He started having supper with Jennifer every night, and the whole time he'd sit there and watch her and make infrequent but agonizing remarks about the brunette.

"Sandy's getting a new colt tomorrow," he mentioned one evening, smiling wistfully. "She asked if I'd come over and look at it for her."

"Can't she see it by herself?" she asked sweetly.

"Conformation is very important in a horse," he said, "I used to breed them years ago, before I got interested in cattle."

"Oh." She concentrated on her food.

"How's the decorating coming?"

"Fine," she said through her teeth. "We're getting the paper up in your bedroom tomorrow. Then there'll only be the other bedrooms to go. You never said how you liked the way the living room and the study came out."

"They're okay," he said. He lifted a forkful of dessert to his mouth and she wanted to jump up and stab him in the lip. Okay! And she'd spent days on the projects, working well into the night alongside the men!

He glanced up at her flushed face. "Wasn't that enthusiastic enough?" He took a sip of coffee. "Damn, Jenny, what a hell of a great job you're doing on the house!" he said with a big, artificial smile, "I'm pleased as punch!"

"I'd like to punch you," she muttered. She slammed down her napkin, slid out of the chair, and stomped out of the room.

Watching her, Everett's eyes narrowed and a faint, predatory smile curved his lips.

The next day, she concentrated on his bedroom. It was difficult to work in there, thinking about whose territory it was. Her eyes kept drifting to the bed where he slept, to the pillow where he laid his dark head. Once she paused beside it and ran her hand loving over the cover. Besotted, she told herself curtly. She was besotted, and it was no use. He was going to marry that skinny, flat-chested brunette!

She didn't even stop for lunch, much less supper. The workmen had left long before, and she was working on the last wall, when Everett came into the room and stood watching her with a cup of coffee in his hand.

"Have you given up eating?" he asked.

"Yep."

He cocked an eyebrow. "Want some coffee?"

"Nope."

He chuckled softly. "Bad imitation. You don't even look like Gary Cooper. You're too short."

She glared down at him. Her jeans were covered with glue. So were her fingers, her bare arms, and the front of her white tee shirt. "Did you want something?"

"Yes. To go to bed. I've got to get an early start in the morning. I'm taking Sandy fishing."

She stared into the bucket of glue and wondered how he'd look plastered to the wall. It was tempting, but dangerous.

"I'd like to finish this one wall," she murmured quietly.

"Go ahead. I'm going to have a shower." He stripped off his shirt. She glanced at him, fascinated by the dark perfection of him, by the ripple of muscle, the way the light played on his skin as he started to take off his . . . *trousers*!

Her eyes jerked back to the glue and her hands trembled. "Everett?" she said in a squeaky voice.

"Well, don't look," he said reasonably. "I can't very well take a bath in my clothes."

"I could have left the room," she said.

"Why? Aren't you curious?" he taunted.

She gritted her teeth. "No!"

"Coward."

She put glue and more glue on a strip of wallpaper until the glue was three times as thick as the paper it was spread on. Not until she heard the shower running did she relax. She put the wallpaper in place and started scrambling down the ladder.

Unfortunately, just because the shower was running, it didn't mean that Everett was in it. She got down and started for the door, and there he stood, with a towel wrapped around his narrow hips and not another stitch on.

"Going somewhere?" he asked.

"Yes. Out of here!" she exclaimed, starting past him.

She never knew exactly how it happened. One minute she was walking toward the door, and the next she was lying flat on the bed with Everett's hard body crushing her into the mattress.

His chest rose and fell slowly, his eyes burned down into hers. Holding her gaze, he eased the towel away and bent to her mouth.

She trembled with kindling passion. It was so incredibly sweet to let her hands run over his hard, warm body, to feel the muscles of his back and arms and shoulders and hips. To let him kiss her softly, with growing intimacy. To know the crush of his body, the blatant force of his hunger for her. To love him with her hands and her mouth.

He lifted his head a minute later and looked into her awed eyes. "You're not so squeaky clean yourself," he said softly. "Why don't you come and take a bath with me?"

Her hands touched his hard arms gently, lovingly. "Because we'd do more than bathe, and you know it," she replied on a soft sigh. "All you have to do is touch me, and you can have anything you want. It's always been like that. The only reason I'm still a virgin is that you haven't insisted."

"Why do you think I haven't?" he prodded.

She shifted. "I don't know. Conscience, maybe?"

He bent and brushed his mouth softly over hers. "Go and put on something soft and pretty. Have a shower. Then come downstairs to the living room and we'll talk."

She swallowed. "I thought you had to get to bed early. To take Sandy fishing," she murmured resentfully.

"Did it ever occur to you that you might be formidable competition for her, if you cared to make the effort?" he asked, watching her. "Or didn't you know how easy it would be to seduce me? And once you did that," he murmured, touching her soft mouth, "I'd probably feel obliged to marry you. Not being on the pill and all," his eyes went back to hers with blazing intensity, "you could get pregnant."

Her breath caught in her throat. She never knew when he was teasing, when he was serious. And now, her mind was whirling.

While she worried over his intentions, he moved

away from her and got to his feet, and she stared at him in helpless fascination.

"You see?" he said, his voice deep and full of secrets, "it isn't so shocking, is it?"

She lifted her eyes to his. "You're . . . very . . ." She tried to find words.

"So are you, honey," he said. "Take your bath and I'll see you downstairs."

And he walked off, oblivious to her intent stare.

Minutes later, she went nervously down the staircase in a white dress, her hair freshly washed and dried, loose around her shoulders. Something that had been brewing between them for a long time was coming abruptly to a head, and she wasn't quite sure how to face it. She had a terrible feeling that he was going to proposition her again, and that she was going to be stupid enough to accept. She loved him madly, wanted him madly. That Sandy person was after him, and Jennifer was afraid. She couldn't quite accept the idea that he might marry someone else. Despite the pain he'd caused her, she dwelled on the fear of losing him.

He was waiting for her. In beige trousers and a patterned beige shirt, he looked larger than life. All man. Sensual and incredibly attractive, especially when she got close enough to catch the scent of his big body.

"Here," he said, offering her a small brandy.

"Thank you," she said politely. She took it, touching his fingers, looking up into dark, quiet eyes. Her lips parted helplessly.

"Now sit down. I want to ask you something."

She sat on the edge of the sofa, but instead of taking the seat beside her, he knelt on the carpet just in front of her. Because of his height, that put her on an unnerving level with his eyes.

"Afraid of me, even now?" he asked softly.

"Especially now," she whispered, trembling. She put the snifter to one side and her trembling fingers reached out and touched the hard lines of his face. "Everett, I'm . . . so very much in love with you," she said, her voice breaking. "If you want me to be your mistress . . . oh!"

She was on the carpet, in his arms, being kissed so hungrily that she couldn't even respond to him. His mouth devoured hers, hurting, bruising, and he trembled all over as if with a fever. His hands trembled as they touched, with expert sureness, every line and curve of her body.

"Say it again," he said roughly, lifting his head just enough to look at her.

Her body ached for his. She leaned toward him helplessly. "I love you," she whispered, pride gone to ashes. "I love you, I love you!"

His head moved down to her bodice, his mouth nudged at the buttons, his hands bit into her back. She reached down blindly to get the fabric out of his way, to give him anything, everything he wanted. There were no more secrets. She belonged to him.

His mouth taught her sensations she'd never dreamed her body would feel. She breathed in gasps as his lips and teeth explored her like some precious delicacy. Her hands held him there, caressed his dark head, loved what he was doing to her.

He raised his head to look at her, smiling faintly at her rapt face, her wide, dark green eyes, her flushed face, the glorious disarray of her hair and her dress.

"I'll remember you like this for the rest of our lives," he said, "the way you look right now, in the first sweet seconds of passion. Do you want me badly?"

"Yes," she confessed. She brought his hand to her body and held it against her taut flesh, brushing his knuckles lazily across it. "Feel?"

His nostrils flared and there was something reckless and unbridled in the eyes that held hers. "For a virgin," he murmured, "you're pretty damned exciting to make love to."

She smiled wildly, hotly. "Teach me."

"Not yet."

"Please."

He shook his head. He sat up, leaning back against the sofa with his long legs stretched out, and looked down at her with a wicked smile. "Fasten your dress. You make me crazy like that."

"I thought that was the whole point of the thing?" she asked unsteadily.

"It was, until you started making declarations of love. I was going to seduce you on the sofa. But now I suppose we'd better do it right."

Her eyes widened in confusion. "I don't under-stand."

He pulled her up and across his lap. "Oh, the hell with it," he murmured, and opened the top button of her bodice again. "God, I love to look at you!"

She swallowed hard. "Don't you want me?"

"Jenny." He laughed. He turned and brought her hips very gently against his. "See?" he whis-pered.

She buried her face in his throat and he rocked her softly, tenderly.

"Then, why?" she asked on a moan.

"Because we have to do things in the right order, honey. First we get married, then we have sex, then we make babies."

She stiffened. "What?"

"Didn't you hear me?" He eased her head down on his arm so that he could see her face.

"But, Sandy . . ." she faltered.

"Sandy is a nice girl," he murmured. "I danced one dance with her, and she went back to her fiancé. He's a nice boy. You'll like him."

"Fiancé!"

He jerked her close and held her hard, roughly. "I love you," he said in a voice that paralyzed her. His eyes blazed with it, burned with it. "Oh, God, I love you, Jenny. Love you, want you, need you, in every single damned way there is! If you want me to get on my knees, I'll do it, I'll do anything to make you forget what I said and did to you that last day you were here." He bent and kissed her hungrily, softly, and lifted his head again, breathing hard. "I knew I loved you then," he said, "when you handed me that check to pay for my bull, and told me the truth. And all I could think of was that I loved you, and that you were out of my reach forever. A career woman, a woman with some money of her own, and I had nothing to offer you, no way to keep you. And I chased you away, because it was torture to look at you and feel that way and have no hope at all."

"Rett!" she burst out. Tears welled up in her eyes and she clung to him. "Oh, Rett, why didn't you tell me? I loved you so much!"

"I didn't know that," he said. His voice shook a little. His arms contracted. "I thought you were playing me along. It wasn't until you left that I realized that you must have cared one hell of a lot, to have done what you did for me." He shifted restlessly, and ground her against him. "Don't you know? Haven't you worked it out yet, why I sold the oil rights? I did it so that I'd have enough money to bring you back."

She caught her breath, and the tears overflowed onto his shirt, his throat.

"I didn't even have the price of a bus ticket." He laughed huskily, his voice tormented with memory. "And I knew that without you, the land wouldn't matter, because I couldn't live. I couldn't stay alive. So I sold the oil rights and I bought a car and I called Sally Wade. And then, I parked across the street to watch for you. And you came out," he said roughly, "laughing and looking so beautiful . . . holding onto that redheaded ass's arm! I could have broken your neck!"

"He was my friend. Nothing more." She nuzzled her face against him. "I thought you wanted revenge. I didn't realize. . . . !"

"I wouldn't let Consuelo touch your room, did she tell you?" he whispered. "I left it the way it was. For the first week or so . . . I could still catch the scent of you on the pillow . . ." His voice broke, and she searched blindly for his mouth, and gave him comfort in the only way she could.

Her fingers touched his face, loved it; her lips told him things, secrets, that even words wouldn't. Gently, tenderly, she drew him up onto the sofa with her, and eased down beside him on it. And with her mouth and her hands and her body, she told him in the sweetest possible way that he'd never be alone as long as she lived.

"We can't," he whispered, trembling.

"Why?" she moaned softly.

"Because I want you in church, Jenny Wren," he whispered, easing her onto her side, soothing her with his hands and his mouth. "I want it all to be just right. I want to hear the words and watch your face when you say them, and tell the whole world that you're my woman. And then," he breathed softly, "then we'll make love and celebrate in the sweetest, most complete way there is. But not like this, darling. Not on a sofa, without the rings or the

words or the beauty of taking our vows together."
He drew back and looked into her damp eyes.
"You'll want that, when you look back on our first
time. You'll want it when the children are old
enough to be told how we met, how we married.
You won't want a tarnished memory to put in your
scrapbook."

She kissed him softly. "Thank you."

"I love you," he said, smiling. "I can wait. If,"
he added with a lift of his eyebrow, "you'll put your
clothes back on and stop trying to lead me into a
life of sin."

"I haven't taken them off," she protested.

"You have." He got up and looked down at her,
with the dress around her waist.

"Well, look at you," she grumbled. His shirt was
off and out of his trousers, and his belt was
unbuckled.

"You did it," he accused.

She burst out laughing as she buttoned buttons.
"I suppose I did. Imagine me, actually trying to
seduce you. And after all the times I accused you of
it!"

"I don't remember complaining," he remarked.

She got to her feet and went into his arms with a
warm sigh. "Me, either. How soon can we get
married?"

"How about Friday?"

"Three days?" she groaned.

"You can take cold showers," he promised her.
"And finish decorating the house. You're not going

to have a lot of time for decorating after we're married."

"I'm not, huh?" she murmured. "What will I be doing?"

"I hoped you might ask," he returned with a smile. He bent his head, lifting her gently in his arms. "This is what you'll be doing." And he kissed her with such tenderness that she felt tears running down her warm cheeks. Since it seemed like such a lovely occupation, she didn't even protest. After all, she'd have plenty of time for decorating when the children started school. Meanwhile, Everett showed promise of being a full-time job.

Silhouette Romance

IT'S YOUR OWN SPECIAL TIME

Contemporary romances for today's women.
Each month, six very special love stories will be yours
from SILHOUETTE.

$1.75 each

☐ 104 Vitek	☐ 131 Stanford	☐ 159 Tracy	☐ 186 Howard
☐ 105 Eden	☐ 132 Wisdom	☐ 160 Hampson	☐ 187 Scott
☐ 106 Dailey	☐ 133 Rowe	☐ 161 Trent	☐ 188 Cork
☐ 107 Bright	☐ 134 Charles	☐ 162 Ashby	☐ 189 Stephens
☐ 108 Hampson	☐ 135 Logan	☐ 163 Roberts	☐ 190 Hampson
☐ 109 Vernon	☐ 136 Hampson	☐ 164 Browning	☐ 191 Browning
☐ 110 Trent	☐ 137 Hunter	☐ 165 Young	☐ 192 John
☐ 111 South	☐ 138 Wilson	☐ 166 Wisdom	☐ 193 Trent
☐ 112 Stanford	☐ 139 Vitek	☐ 167 Hunter	☐ 194 Barry
☐ 113 Browning	☐ 140 Erskine	☐ 168 Carr	☐ 195 Dailey
☐ 114 Michaels	☐ 142 Browning	☐ 169 Scott	☐ 196 Hampson
☐ 115 John	☐ 143 Roberts	☐ 170 Ripy	☐ 197 Summers
☐ 116 Lindley	☐ 144 Goforth	☐ 171 Hill	☐ 198 Hunter
☐ 117 Scott	☐ 145 Hope	☐ 172 Browning	☐ 199 Roberts
☐ 118 Dailey	☐ 146 Michaels	☐ 173 Camp	☐ 200 Lloyd
☐ 119 Hampson	☐ 147 Hampson	☐ 174 Sinclair	☐ 201 Starr
☐ 120 Carroll	☐ 148 Cork	☐ 175 Jarrett	☐ 202 Hampson
☐ 121 Langan	☐ 149 Saunders	☐ 176 Vitek	☐ 203 Browning
☐ 122 Scofield	☐ 150 Major	☐ 177 Dailey	☐ 204 Carroll
☐ 123 Sinclair	☐ 151 Hampson	☐ 178 Hampson	☐ 205 Maxam
☐ 124 Beckman	☐ 152 Halston	☐ 179 Beckman	☐ 206 Manning
☐ 125 Bright	☐ 153 Dailey	☐ 180 Roberts	☐ 207 Windham
☐ 126 St. George	☐ 154 Beckman	☐ 181 Terrill	☐ 208 Halston
☐ 127 Roberts	☐ 155 Hampson	☐ 182 Clay	☐ 209 LaDame
☐ 128 Hampson	☐ 156 Sawyer	☐ 183 Stanley	☐ 210 Eden
☐ 129 Converse	☐ 157 Vitek	☐ 184 Hardy	☐ 211 Walters
☐ 130 Hardy	☐ 158 Reynolds	☐ 185 Hampson	☐ 212 Young

$1.95 each

☐ 213 Dailey	☐ 219 Cork	☐ 225 St. George	☐ 231 Dailey
☐ 214 Hampson	☐ 220 Hampson	☐ 226 Hampson	☐ 232 Hampson
☐ 215 Roberts	☐ 221 Browning	☐ 227 Beckman	☐ 233 Vernon
☐ 216 Saunders	☐ 222 Carroll	☐ 228 King	☐ 234 Smith
☐ 217 Vitek	☐ 223 Summers	☐ 229 Thornton	☐ 235 James
☐ 218 Hunter	☐ 224 Langan	☐ 230 Stevens	☐ 236 Maxam

Silhouette Romance

$1.95 each

☐ 237 Wilson	☐ 262 John	☐ 287 Joyce	☐ 312 Vernon
☐ 238 Cork	☐ 263 Wilson	☐ 288 Smith	☐ 313 Rainville
☐ 239 McKay	☐ 264 Vine	☐ 289 Saunders	☐ 314 Palmer
☐ 240 Hunter	☐ 265 Adams	☐ 290 Hunter	☐ 315 Smith
☐ 241 Wisdom	☐ 266 Trent	☐ 291 McKay	☐ 316 Macomber
☐ 242 Brooke	☐ 267 Chase	☐ 292 Browning	☐ 317 Langan
☐ 243 Saunders	☐ 268 Hunter	☐ 293 Morgan	☐ 318 Herrington
☐ 244 Sinclair	☐ 269 Smith	☐ 294 Cockcroft	☐ 319 Lloyd
☐ 245 Trent	☐ 270 Camp	☐ 295 Vernon	☐ 320 Brooke
☐ 246 Carroll	☐ 271 Allison	☐ 296 Paige	☐ 321 Glenn
☐ 247 Halldorson	☐ 272 Forrest	☐ 297 Young	☐ 322 Hunter
☐ 248 St. George	☐ 273 Beckman	☐ 298 Hunter	☐ 323 Browning
☐ 249 Scofield	☐ 274 Roberts	☐ 299 Roberts	☐ 324 Maxam
☐ 250 Hampson	☐ 275 Browning	☐ 300 Stephens	☐ 325 Smith
☐ 251 Wilson	☐ 276 Vernon	☐ 301 Palmer	☐ 326 Lovan
☐ 252 Roberts	☐ 277 Wilson	☐ 302 Smith	☐ 327 James
☐ 253 James	☐ 278 Hunter	☐ 303 Langan	☐ 328 Palmer
☐ 254 Palmer	☐ 279 Ashby	☐ 304 Cork	☐ 329 Broadrick
☐ 255 Smith	☐ 280 Roberts	☐ 305 Browning	☐ 330 Ferrell
☐ 256 Hampson	☐ 281 Lovan	☐ 306 Gordon	☐ 331 Michaels
☐ 257 Hunter	☐ 282 Halldorson	☐ 307 Wildman	☐ 332 McCarty
☐ 258 Ashby	☐ 283 Payne	☐ 308 Young	☐ 333 Page
☐ 259 English	☐ 284 Young	☐ 309 Hardy	
☐ 260 Martin	☐ 285 Gray	☐ 310 Hunter	
☐ 261 Saunders	☐ 286 Cork	☐ 311 Gray	

Silhouette Romance